A DEADLY COMBINATION

Dean sat up straighter in his chair and his gaze became intent as he watched the other man. Three times Leonard spun the dial to the left. Then, as he spun it to the right he murmured, "Twenty—once, twice, three times—" He spun it twice more to the right: "Sixty-five—" He spun it a third time, once: "Thirteen—" He spun the dial to the left again and the door swung open.

Dean found himself memorizing the combination, not knowing why he did it, not wanting to do it, breaking out in a nervous sweat because he couldn't stop himself from doing it.

Leonard unlocked the drawer, lifted it out, and set it on a table. He removed a stack of crisp green bonds from it, took his passport out from under them, replaced the bonds in the drawer, put it back in the safe, locked it, closed the safe, spun the dial, returned the key to his desk . . .

The whole episode had consumed only three or four minutes, but Dean discovered that he was shaking all over, the ice in his glass tinkling against the sides of it, his hand was so unsteady.

Leonard, absorbed in his own affairs, didn't notice how quiet Dean had become . . .

DORIS MILES DISNEY
THE LAST STRAW

ZEBRA BOOKS
KENSINGTON PUBLISHING CORP.

ZEBRA BOOKS

are published by

Kensington Publishing Corp.
475 Park Avenue South
New York, NY 10016

First printing: February 1988

Printed in the United States of America

For AUNTY,
my dear fellow writer of the purple sage

One

The Colebrook Arms with solid dignity proclaimed the financial standing of its tenants. It was set back out of reach of such street noises as its select neighborhood permitted. The lawn in front of it was already, in the first half of April, a green velvet carpet ornamented with beds of tulips coming into bloom; the fountain in the flagstoned courtyard had been turned on to spray water over a group of marble maidens lounging in a marble saucer. The maidens were decorously clothed; there was nothing about them to shock the most prudish of the elderly ladies who were numbered among the tenants of the Colebrook Arms and who passed the fountain every day. It was in keeping with the restraint that prevailed throughout the structure and the grounds around it.

Dean Lipscomb, new in the city of Hampton, was impressed with the Colebrook Arms when he saw it for the first time on an evening in April. He parked his car, a 1946 Plymouth, in the driveway that ran around the building and walked slowly toward the main entrance, looking around him with a gaze both appreciative and envious.

"Elaine would like it," he thought. "It would suit her right down to the ground. If she could have a place like this maybe she wouldn't complain so much about coming to live in Hampton."

But there wasn't, Dean knew, the remotest prospect of Elaine and him renting an apartment at the Colebrook Arms. The very smallest of them would probably run well over a hundred a month and he, in his new job with Beecher and Company, Investment Brokers, was earning seventy-five dollars a week. Of course that was only while he was learning the business, Tad Beecher said. Even so, it would be a long time before he could hope to install Elaine in an apartment at the Colebrook Arms.

He studied the name plates in the vestibule. Leonard Riggott, his prospective host, lived on the third floor. He pushed the bell beside his name and presently the buzzer sounded, opening the door to the lobby.

The lobby was small. There was no doorman. Hampton, Dean reminded himself, wasn't New York or Philadelphia. It appeared that even its plushiest places didn't employ doormen. If you were seeking information about someone in the building, you rang the superintendent's bell.

There was a self-service elevator. He stepped into it, pressed the button for the third floor, and was carried up to it.

Leonard Riggott lived in a front apartment near the elevator. He opened the door and greeted Dean benignly.

"Well, young fellow, you're right on time. It's just

six-thirty. I'm the one who's late. Come in." He stood back to allow Dean to enter the foyer. He was wearing a bathrobe and his bare feet were thrust into leather scuffs. "I got tied up downtown and was so late getting home that I'm just this minute out of the shower. But come along to the den and have a drink while I get dressed."

The foyer led to an enormous living room with a wood-burning fireplace, built-in cabinets and bookshelves, and fine modern furniture. There was a wall of windows across the front and more windows in the end wall with a doorway to their right.

Leonard, a bachelor of fifty with a face whose handsomeness had faded, a body gone soft with easy living, hard eyes and a ready smile, led the young man through the doorway, along a hall past a lavatory and a small kitchen to the den at the end of the hall. His bedroom and bathroom lay beyond the den.

He went to a portable bar and asked Dean what he would have to drink.

"Bourbon and water."

Leonard mixed the drink, handed it to his guest, and disappeared into the bedroom to dress.

Dean settled himself in a chair and looked about him. The room was done in warm shades of brown accented with rust and yellow. It contained a wall safe, a filing cabinet, a large desk, a sofa and easy chairs. It was a comfortable room, a man's room, just right, Dean thought, for bringing in a friend or two to sit down and talk while you had a few drinks. Riggott was lucky. He and his kind seemed to have all the luck, all the money. Dean would have to content himself with some hole in the wall that would be furnished with the

9

dregs of a secondhand store.

He wished Elaine could see this place. No, he didn't. It would only sharpen her discontent with what he could give her.

He sighed and drank his bourbon. Thoughts of Elaine were accompanied by a sinking feeling in his stomach that had become all too familiar in the past year. He was losing her. Week by week, month by month, she was retreating from him; and as he saw this happen his love for her swelled and grew and took overriding possession of him. . . .

They had been married three years. He had proposed to her five times before she accepted him. Her acceptance came after he had been called back on active duty from the Air Force Reserve, in which he held a first lieutenant's rank. He had been sent to North Africa, where Elaine could have joined him during the twenty months he was stationed there but hadn't. In the year and a half since his return she had become ever less satisfied with being married to him. They'd had a slow start, of course, and then that bad break with the insurance agency where he'd been employed in Philadelphia. But she hadn't known the details of that; she thought he'd lost his job because they were cutting down on personnel.

Now he was making a fresh start in Hampton. His father, on a trip to New York, had run into Tad Beecher, an old college classmate, and spoken to him about a job for his son. Tad had said he could make a place for him at Beecher's, and Dean's father had been delighted. Delighted and relieved. He wanted Dean out of Philadelphia.

But so far Elaine had stayed on there, moving back

home with her parents, keeping her job, showing no enthusiasm about living in Hampton, seemingly not missing him, certainly not with the aching sense of loss that Dean felt away from her. . . .

While he drank his bourbon, Leonard was back and forth between the bedroom and den, coming out with lather on his face to talk about his golf score that morning, and again, when he was nearly dressed, about his plans for taking a trip somewhere.

He, too, had been a college classmate of Dean's father. He lived on inherited money and kept a close watch on his investments. Tad Beecher was his broker. He was at Beecher's frequently and had begun to show a friendly interest in Dean. Twice lately he had taken the young man to lunch; tonight was the first time he had invited him to dine with him at his club.

He traveled a good deal, Dean knew. He was as free as air, he had the money to go anywhere he pleased. He was one of the lucky people.

Dean's expression turned moody as he reflected on Leonard's luck. He had none himself—except in having persuaded Elaine to marry him. But nowadays it looked as if he were going to lose her. Elaine, lovely, unreachable, wanted far more than he could give her. She had every right to expect far more. . . .

His moody expression deepened. He emptied his glass and set it down.

Leonard Riggott finished dressing and came into the room. He was all affability. "Well, young fellow, let's have another drink before we go, eh?"

Dean watched him with veiled resentment while he mixed the drinks. If he himself had just a fraction of Riggott's money, enough to buy Elaine the diamond

11

she'd never had, the car of her own she talked about so much, clothes like the Italian-original cocktail dress she'd admired in the window of a Chestnut Street shop last week end when he was in Philadelphia with her; if he had enough money for these things, he could make Elaine happy.

He accepted his refilled glass from Leonard and thought of saying to him, "Look, Mr. Riggott, how about a little private philanthropy? Say, ten thousand dollars' worth? To bolster up my marriage and give my wife and me a real start. We're young, I've lost a lot of time in service, I need some help—"

The older man had seated himself opposite him. The hard blue of his eyes didn't soften as he smiled at Dean, raised his glass, and said, "Well, here's to you."

His smile would vanish fast, Dean reflected sardonically, if he asked him for money, ten dollars or ten thousand. Riggott, from what he knew of him, was the type to spend his money freely only on himself.

Dean smiled back at him and raised his glass to his lips. He was a conventionally good-looking young man with wavy brown hair, brown eyes, and regular features. But when he stopped smiling his mouth fell into the same moody lines it had had before.

Making conversation, he said, "That trip you mentioned, Mr. Riggott—where do you think you'll go?"

"I haven't decided yet. Just away for a few months. Sometimes, Dean, absenting yourself from your usual haunts solves a lot of problems."

"I suppose so." The young man couldn't resist adding, "But it takes money."

"Yes." Leonard swirled the ice in his drink and

12

watched the bubbles rise. "However—"

When he didn't continue Dean asked, "North America, South America, Europe, Asia, Africa, Australia? Do you take out an atlas and go eeny, meeny, miney, mo?"

Leonard laughed. "Not quite like that. But say, that reminds me—" He set down his glass and got to his feet. "While I think of it I must get my passport out. I'll be going downtown in the morning and I can drop it off at the Watson agency and they'll get it renewed for me."

He went to the safe in the wall. "I keep it in here—"

Dean sat up straighter in his chair and his gaze became intent as he watched the other man. Three times Leonard spun the dial to the left. Then, as he spun it to the right he murmured, "Twenty—once, twice, three times—" He spun it twice more to the right: "Sixty-five—" He spun it a third time, once: "Thirteen—" He spun the dial to the left again and the door swung open.

Dean found himself memorizing the combination, not knowing why he did it, not wanting to do it, breaking out in a nervous sweat because he couldn't stop himself from doing it.

It was a small safe. Over the older man's shoulder he could see bundles of papers in the compartments and the locked center drawer.

Leonard took a key to the drawer from his desk. "I don't keep much in here," he said, as if in explanation of Dean's silent conjecture over how little the safe held. "Most of my stuff is in safe deposit. But I keep my passport handy and insurance papers and some government threes—I don't like clipping coupons at the bank—and whenever I buy stock I stick the

13

certificates in here until I get around to putting them in my box. So a safe is a convenience for me."

"I can see where it would be," said Dean, who had no valuables to keep either in a safe or at a bank. "When do you clip the coupons on your threes?"

"In March and September." Leonard unlocked the drawer, lifted it out, and set it on a table. He removed a stack of crisp green bonds from it, took his passport out from under them, replaced the bonds in the drawer, put it back in the safe, locked it, closed the safe, spun the dial, returned the key to his desk. . . .

The whole episode had consumed only three or four minutes, but Dean discovered that he was shaking all over, the ice in his glass tinkling against the sides of it, his hand was so unsteady. He set the glass down and, to give himself something to do, took out his pipe and penknife. The commonplace actions of scraping the bowl of the pipe, filling it with tobacco, and lighting it restored his self-possession.

Leonard, after placing his passport on the desk where he would see it in the morning, returned to his chair and picked up the conversation where he had dropped it to open the safe. Absorbed in his own affairs, he was not particularly observant of other people's behavior. He didn't notice how quiet Dean had become all at once.

They finished their drinks and drove in Leonard's new Jaguar to his club, where they were to have dinner. Dean made mental comparisons between it and his own old Plymouth and felt his dislike of the older man increase.

But under the influence of a good dinner his mood improved. Leonard stopped talking about himself and turned the conversation to Dean's future.

"You've made a fine connection there," he said, referring to Beecher and Company. "Tad's the best there is—no doubt your father told you that—and he seems to be taking a real interest in you."

"Yes, I know," Dean replied, infusing his tone with the gratitude that was expected of him. "He and Mrs. Beecher have been wonderful to me. Right now she's hunting for an apartment for my wife and me. So far, though, no luck."

"Zatso? There've been so many new apartment houses going up I shouldn't think you'd have much trouble."

"I wouldn't, probably, if I could pay their prices." Dean's tone was dry. "But after all, I'm making a pretty small start at Beecher's."

"Well, you'll do better later on. A little hardship when you're young won't do you any harm." Leonard spoke in the comfortable accents of one born with a silver spoon in his mouth who had never known what it meant to lack anything money could buy.

"I guess not." Dean lowered his gaze to hide the fresh access of dislike in it. "But there are times—"

The older man wasn't interested in Dean's financial difficulties. He changed the subject by inquiring, "When is your wife going to come on?"

"When I find a place for us to live," Dean said briefly. The new subject was the sorest one of all to him.

Leonard, not heeding his tone, became jovial. "I'm anxious to meet her. What are you doing, keeping her hidden away from your bachelor friends? Tad and Phoebe tell me she's a real beauty."

"She's been in Hampton only once," Dean told him,

forcing a smile. "Next time she's here I'll see that you meet her."

"Yes, you must. Perhaps we can arrange it for both of you to have dinner with me. I hope it will be before I go away."

"How long do you expect to be gone?"

Leonard shrugged. "No idea. Two or three months, perhaps." He gave Dean a knowing look. "Depends on what I find to interest me. But the older I get, the shorter my interest span seems to be."

"Jaded appetite," the younger man commented smilingly. "You've lived too high on the hog too long, Mr. Riggott."

Leonard chuckled and shook his head. "I've had my problems though, just like everyone else."

But not financial ones, Dean said to himself. Or what they could bring one: the nagging, incessant fear of losing the wife you adored because she was getting fed up with shoestring living. You've had none of that, Mr. Riggott.

He was silent, remembering what his father had said about the man opposite him. While his father had been working his way through college, Riggott had been throwing money around, the prototype of his raccoon-coat generation. Tad Beecher had fitted in between the two extremes Dean's father and Leonard Riggott represented. . . .

In the club lounge after dinner the young man was introduced to several of the other members. They seemed like peas in a pod to him, with the same aura of money that surrounded his host and the same assurance that money brings. "His father and I were college classmates," Leonard said in introducing Dean.

16

We were friends, his tone implied. But they hadn't been. Leonard had barely known that Dean's father existed.

Someone suggested a rubber of bridge. "Don't feel like it," Leonard said. "I think we'll go back to my place and have a drink and sit around awhile. That suit you, Dean?" Belatedly he consulted his guest's preference.

"Anything you say, Mr. Riggott."

When they arrived back at the apartment they settled themselves in the den. That was what Dean wanted. He could sit and gaze at the safe. It drew his eyes irresistibly.

The older man mixed drinks, dropped into a chair, and began to tell Dean about the men he had met at the club. This one was president of such-and-such a firm; that one was chairman of the board of such-and-such a bank; another one was senior partner in such-and-such a law firm. And so forth.

Dean pretended to listen and thought about the bonds in the safe. Riggott had said he clipped coupons from them in March and September; September was five months away. There was a stack of them. Government threes payable to bearer. They were probably worth thousands of dollars. Payable to bearer.

His whole being was concentrated on the green pieces of paper that were so tantalizingly near. He thought of what Elaine and he could do if they had them. First of all, get out of this one-horse town. (The Chamber of Commerce would have taken issue with him on this; Hampton's population was close to the quarter-million mark.) Get a real start on his own, not through the patronage of his father's old classmate. Get

17

a new car. One for himself, one for Elaine. Buy her a diamond, the engagement ring she'd never had. Buy her that dress she'd admired last week end. Buy her the earth. How many bonds were there in that safe?

The telephone rang. It was on the desk. Leonard leaned sidewise and scooped up the receiver. He said, "Hello?" His face darkened at the sound of the voice at the other end of the wire. It was a woman's voice. Dean could tell that much about it as it spoke emphatically and at length, giving Leonard the chance to say no more than, "But really— But— But—" Finally there was a pause and he said, "Look, I have someone here— No, it isn't—a young man from Philadelphia. . . . No, I can't. . . . No, don't you even think of such a thing."

His face was set in exasperated lines, his tone was angry. Dean made a guess that the woman who was calling was the problem the other man had mentioned earlier that would be solved by his going away for a while. When he was tired of a woman it seemed that he would lose no time in taking steps to rid himself of her. But either because of Dean's presence, or because he was planning to put himself out of her reach soon and in the meantime wanted to avoid as many scenes with her as he could, Leonard was, at the moment, trying to placate her. At last he said, "All right, I'll run down. But I can't stay a minute. As I told you, I have a guest."

He hung up and summoned a smile for Dean's benefit. "That was a Mrs. Madler who lives on the first floor here," he said. "She needs my advice on something. Do you mind if I just run down? It'll take only a few minutes to straighten it out."

"You go right ahead," Dean replied. "In fact, I can go along home now if you like."

"No, no, you mustn't." Leonard was determined to display his control over the situation downstairs. "Mix yourself another drink and find something to read. I'll be right back."

A moment later he was gone, leaving Dean alone with the safe, which he had said he didn't use often. He had clipped coupons last month, he wouldn't be clipping them again until September. He had taken out his passport, it lay on his desk. He was going away for several months. By the time he returned and discovered his loss it would be June or July. He would have forgotten, or at least the lapse of time would have blurred his memory of tonight, when Dean had heard him murmuring aloud the combination of the safe and seen him take the key to it from his desk. He would have to assume that a burglar had got into his apartment, worked out the combination, and stolen the bonds while he was away.

These thoughts raced through Dean's mind. He stood up, a slight figure of only average height, a rigid figure drawn step by step to the safe, saying in a whisper, "Twenty, three times; sixty-five, twice; thirteen, once."

Two

There were thirty-two thousand-dollar bonds in the safe. Dean's trembling fingers riffled them. Thirty-two thousand dollars . . .

There was also a stock certificate of the Atlantic Telephone and Telegraph Company dated April 2, certifying that Leonard Riggott was the owner of forty shares of the company's stock.

Dean made calculations. Atlantic was selling at one hundred and eighty dollars a share; forty times that was seven thousand, two hundred.

He could hire a safe-deposit box, put the certificate away for a while, and then sell it on the black market.

Common sense dictated returning the certificate to the safe. But it represented too much money. Sooner or later, he told himself, he could unload it, perhaps at half its face value, at least for one third of it.

He added the certificate to the stack of bonds, put the drawer back in place, locked it, and closed the safe. He worked fast but used meticulous care in wiping with a handkerchief every incriminating surface his fingers touched. In the desk drawer from which he had taken the key he found an envelope large enough to hold the bonds and the certificate. But it made a noticeable bulge in his pocket, and besides, he was feverishly anxious to get it out of the apartment. He looked at his watch. The theft had taken only eight minutes; Riggott wouldn't be back just yet. There was time to run downstairs and lock up the bonds in his car.

He set the catch on the foyer door so that he could gain entrance on his return and hurried out of the apartment. He didn't wait for the elevator. He ran down the two flights of stairs to the lobby and out of the building to his car.

There was a tin of tobacco in the glove compartment. Dean thrust it in his pocket. It would serve as an excuse for his absence if Leonard got back to the apartment first.

In the vestibule he had to press three bells at random before a buzzer released the catch on the door. The elevator was in use, the arrow indicating it was at the fourth floor on its way up. The stairs would be quicker. He took them two at a time, but still he found himself too late. Leonard was at his door, taking out his keys.

"It's not locked, Mr. Riggott," Dean called. "I ran out of tobacco, went down to my car to get some, and set the latch so I could get in again."

The older man turned and looked at him with surprise and displeasure. "I never go out and leave my door unlocked. It's a foolhardy practice."

"Oh, I didn't know you felt like that. I'm awfully sorry. I'm not very careful about doors myself and I didn't give a thought to what I was doing. I wasn't gone very long though. Just down to my car and back."

Leonard was unappeased. "I have things that are valuable lying around loose," he said stiffly. "I have to make it a point to be careful about doors."

"I'm awfully sorry," Dean repeated. He followed his host into the apartment, still explaining and apologizing, expressing relief, after they had looked around, that nothing seemed to have been disturbed.

On the whole, he was thinking, it might be just as well that Riggott knew about the interval when his door stood on latch. Months later, discovering the loss of the bonds, he would remember it and tell the police about it. They would reason that a thief had got in, taken an impression of the lock, had a key made, and then, while Riggott was away, opened the safe. It would be strange coincidence, of course, that a chance thief turned out to be an expert safe-cracker—but on the other hand, the chance thief could have known someone who was.

Leonard, now mollified, took Dean back to the den. There the latter had to curb his urgent desire to be gone and a tendency equally urgent to stare at the safe. He made conversation for what seemed like an endless period of time but was in reality only twenty minutes or so. Then he glanced at his watch and said, "Lord, it's ten-thirty already. I'd better be going, Mr. Riggott. I have a couple of letters to write when I get home."

The older man suggested a drink for the road, but Dean refused. His nervousness had reached such a pitch that he had to leave without delay. He felt as if he couldn't draw another breath in the same room with Leonard Riggott and his safe.

This was Dean's first real theft. He didn't count what had happened at the insurance agency in Philadelphia;

after all, his father had made that good. . . .

He thanked Leonard effusively for his hospitality—the latter, he had learned during their short acquaintance, liked an elaborate show of gratitude for any kindnesses he extended—and apologized again for his lack of thought in leaving the door unlocked. Leonard assured him no harm had been done and then the two, the robber and the robbed, parted on the best of terms.

Dean didn't sleep well that night. He dozed and dreamed, confused dreams from which he would awaken with a start, his hand going under the pillow to touch the envelope that held the bonds.

In the morning he locked it in his car again. He couldn't leave it in his room, where it might be found by the landlady or one of the other roomers.

He went to work at nine o'clock, tired, edgy, afraid. His fear mounted as the day wore on. Every moment he expected Leonard to appear and denounce him. Last night in his mad yielding to temptation he had glossed over the importance of the stock certificate being in the safe. Today he felt certain Leonard would decide to take it to his box at the bank. He would open the safe, unlock the drawer—

Thus Dean tormented himself. But the other man didn't appear and there was no word from him. That night Dean tried to think of some way of getting into the apartment and restoring the bonds to the safe; the only thing he could think of was to go to Leonard, confess what he had done, and hand the bonds back to him.

He remembered Leonard's hard eyes, the lack of genuine warmth beneath his affable exterior. He would show no understanding. If he could be persuaded to keep his silence, he would, at the very least, demand that Dean leave Hampton immediately.

That would mean another job gone, a deeper cloud over him; to Elaine it might well be the last straw. . . .

For the next two nights Dean slept with the bonds under his pillow and locked them in his car during the day. He knew this procedure was the height of folly, but he had no better hiding place. He had only his room, his desk at Beecher's, or his car. He didn't dare rent a safe-deposit box in Hampton or nearby. If Leonard found out the bonds were missing, the police would start looking for a safe-deposit box in Dean's name right away.

By the time Thursday came, Dean was regaining his nerve. The theory that had led him into stealing the bonds seemed plausible again. Riggott was busy with plans for his trip and wouldn't get around to taking the Atlantic certificate to the bank. It would slip his mind entirely, Dean told himself. After all, considering how much money the man had, one stock certificate wouldn't loom large in his life.

At ten o'clock that Thursday morning Dean decided to go ahead with the plan he had been forming. He went to Tad Beecher. "I've got the worst headache and feeling of nausea," he announced. "Would you mind if I knocked off for the day and went home to bed?"

Tad was all sympathy. Certainly Dean should go home if he didn't feel well. Shouldn't he see a doctor on the way?

"Maybe I will," Dean told him.

Away from Beecher's, he hurried to his car and headed it through Hampton to the Wilbur Cross

Parkway. He was going to New York.

At one o'clock he was there, walking into the Madison Avenue Trust Company. He had picked that bank because in its bond department a young man was employed who had served with Dean in the Air Force in North America. Dean and he had more or less kept in touch with each other since that time and now Dean needed his good offices.

His first action was to rent a safe-deposit box. He still had a Pennsylvania driver's license. He used it, along with various other papers, to identify himself and gave his father's address as his. Connecticut, his occupation there, could not be permitted to come into the picture.

When he was in possession of a box, he set aside four of the bonds and put the rest of them and the stock certificate in it.

He went next to the bond department to look up his Air Force friend and after handshakes and an exchange of greetings they went out for a drink.

"What are you doing these days?" the friend asked when they were seated in a bar.

No mention of Connecticut, above all, no mention of Beecher and Company. He'd been with an insurance agency in Philadelphia until just recently, Dean replied. But it wasn't what he wanted. Now he was looking around for something else.

In North Africa he had given the impression that he came from a wealthy family. It smoothed the way for him to bring up the matter of four bonds he wanted to sell. When they returned to the bank his friend made no difficulties about arranging to cash them for him.

Presently Dean said good-by and left, his shabby wallet bulging with a thick, wonderful wad of hundred-dollar bills.

He stopped at a leather-goods shop on Madison Avenue to buy himself a new wallet. He was imbued with a feeling of reckless well-being as he left it. He was halfway to Philadelphia already, he reflected. Tomorrow, Good Friday, was a holiday. He might as well go on. He had no clothes with him, but he could remedy that easily enough by buying a few things. He'd need something to put them in, though. He turned back to the leather-goods shop. All his luggage was falling apart. He might as well buy himself a good cowhide bag while he was at it.

Two hours later his shopping was completed, his wallet less bulging than it had been. A diamond ring for Elaine that had cost five hundred dollars was in his pocket and, in the nature of an extra gift, a token of particular thoughtfulness, a tiny gold car with movable wheels to be added to the charm bracelet that had been his engagement gift to her. Elaine wanted a car of her own; she talked a great deal about how much she wanted one. She must regard the new charm for her bracelet as an earnest of his good intentions in that respect. As he set out for Philadelphia his heart sang with anticipation of seeing her and of her changed attitude toward him because of the gifts he brought.

His tracks were well covered, he thought. Phoebe Beecher had invited him to Easter Sunday dinner and he had had to call her to cancel the engagement. He knew the telephone number and the call went through without the operator saying New York was calling. He told Phoebe he felt much better and had decided to

26

drive to Philadelphia to spend the week end with Elaine. He hoped she wouldn't mind that he wouldn't be at her house for Sunday dinner.

"Not a bit," Phoebe assured him. "Are you sure, though, you're well enough to make that long trip? Tad just got home and said you were sick. I was going to call your landlady to see how you were."

"Oh, I'm fine now. I slept all day and I feel better just at the thought of seeing Elaine."

"Of course you do," kindhearted Phoebe agreed. "It's not right for married people to be separated the way you are."

"The minute I find a place for us we'll be together again." Dean felt he could afford to speak with confidence. He had money now with which to make Elaine happy. He added, "I certainly wouldn't expect her to live in a furnished room with me."

"No indeed," said Phoebe, who would herself have lived in a tent with Tad rather than be apart from him. "Well, have a nice week end."

"Thank you, I'm sure I will," Dean replied.

His happiness increased as mile after mile of the New Jersey Turnpike fell behind him. He had stopped worrying about Leonard. Through cashing four of the bonds and spending nearly seven hundred dollars of the money he received for them, and through putting the rest of them in safe deposit, he felt that he had put his stamp of ownership on them. They were no longer stolen bonds, they belonged to him.

He would explain his sudden affluence to Elaine by telling her he'd taken a little flyer on the market; then, to pave the way for the future, he'd say he meant to try his luck again.

Next week he'd get rid of this old heap he was driving. Not to buy a new car. He wouldn't be foolish enough to make that kind of display, not with Tad Beecher knowing or at least able to make a shrewd guess that Dean had had little or nothing when he arrived in Hampton three months ago. But he could come a little closer to owning a new model. He'd buy a '51 or a '52.

His thoughts turned to Elaine and how excited she'd be when he brought out his gifts for her.

While Dean was on his way to his wife Leonard Riggott sat at his desk writing an air-mail letter to an old friend, Arthur Waite, in Vancouver, accepting the invitation he had received from him in the morning mail to come out to Vancouver the end of the month for two or three weeks' fishing.

The invitation had changed Leonard's plans. He wouldn't go to Italy after all. It would be filling up with tourists in a few weeks, and anyway, he didn't feel particularly like going. He'd drive out to Vancouver and after the fishing trip he'd go to California and avail himself of Hank Wilson's standing invitation to visit him at his ranch in the San Fernando Valley.

Leonard wrote that he would plan to start for Vancouver in about ten days and would wire the expected date of his arrival. He had a sense of satisfaction when he finished the letter and dropped it in the mail chute in the hall. His new plans would keep him away for at least two months. That would give Loretta ample time to climb down off her high horse and accept the fact that he had no intention of marrying her, that their affair was at an end. He would not tolerate from any woman the kinds of scenes she

28

had been making lately, accusing him of doing her a great wrong. That was ridiculous. She was well over forty, a divorcée, and she had gone into the thing with her eyes open, knowing full well that he was not matrimonially inclined. No doubt she had felt she could change his attitude. Well, she'd found out she was mistaken; she had overrated her charms.

He looked at his watch when he was back in his apartment. Six o'clock. Time to shower and dress for his dinner date with Dotty Lanford, the widow he had met two months ago at a party at the golf club. A charming little creature, he reflected, as he moved along the hall toward his bedroom. Sensible, too—or so she seemed at this stage of their acquaintance. Only time would tell about that, of course. . . .

The next week passed quickly for Leonard. He was busy sorting his fishing gear, dropping in at Clinton's sporting-goods store to add to it, going to the bank for traveler's checks, attending a bachelor dinner for a fellow club member, taking Dotty Lanford to a concert, spending an evening with Glenn Saxton, his nephew and heir, and telling him about his projected trip and that he would keep him informed of his whereabouts.

He didn't drop in at Beecher's that week as he usually did. But on Thursday he phoned Tad and told him he was going away. Then he said, "I've been thinking over what you said about Amalgamated Chemical, Tad. If it drops below ninety, pick me up a couple of hundred shares of it, will you? Get in touch with Glenn if you do buy it for me. He'll have my address and he'll let me know so I can send you a check."

"Okay," Tad replied. "I'll take care of it."

On Friday Leonard went downtown. Watson's Travel Agency had called to tell him his passport had come back from the State Department and he stopped to pick it up. Then he went to Parker's, Jeweler's, to look for a present for Dotty Lanford, whose birthday was tomorrow. He couldn't make up his mind what to buy her. The bracelet he liked best cost more than he was prepared to spend on her at the present time. He wanted to be certain of receiving full value for his money and thus far Dotty was keeping him at a distance. He'd think about the bracelet, he said, and let them know in the morning.

When he got home he took his passport to the safe to put it away. He wouldn't be needing it on his trip.

After the first stunned interval of staring disbelievingly into the empty drawer Leonard thought, "I must call the police." But at his desk, his hand reaching for the receiver, he paused. His mind had begun to function again. Dean Lipscomb had been in this room with him last week when he opened the safe. He thought about what it meant, his habit of repeating the combination aloud, his getting the key from his desk in front of the young man, and later in the evening leaving him alone in the apartment while he went downstairs to head Loretta off from coming up and making a scene in front of Dean.

He remembered meeting Dean in the hall on his return and the flimsy excuse advanced by the latter for going out to his car. He, all unsuspecting, had accepted it, and Dean had had the hardihood to sit down in this very room with him and carry on a conversation before he went away with the bonds.

The stock certificate—he had taken that too. What

good would it do him? Did he have some way of cashing in on it?

"God," Leonard said aloud. "Who'd believe he was such a scoundrel?"

Deeply shaken as he was, he went on reconstructing what had happened, his own ready talk about how little he used the safe and Dean's question about when he clipped coupons.

The young man had felt secure in what he did. He knew Leonard was going away and had counted on months going by—as well they might have—before he found out about his loss. No doubt Dean had intended to be far away by that time—or had he hoped Leonard would have forgotten about opening the safe in front of him and would think the bonds were stolen while he was on his trip?

Leonard sat tapping his fingers on the desk. What was he going to do about it?

He wasn't inclined to call the police immediately. He would look a fool telling them the circumstances of the theft, how he had practically given Dean Lipscomb a gilt-edged invitation to steal the bonds from him.

It would be in all the newspapers. He'd never hear the end of it at the club.

There was Tad to be considered too. He seized on the thought of Tad, one of his oldest friends. Exposure of Dean would undermine confidence in Beecher and Company. He didn't want that. He didn't want to hurt Tad, who had taken Dean under his wing in all good faith.

What should he do then?

He thought of Jim O'Neill, Hampton County detective. Jim had a summer place next door to his at

31

High Point Lake. Why couldn't he dump the whole thing in Jim's lap?

No, he thought next, he wouldn't go straight to Jim. The latter would probably recommend bringing the police in on it without the least delay.

That wouldn't do. It would get in the papers. What a fool he would look!

Wasn't there another way of handling it? What if he summoned Dean to his apartment, laid the facts before him, and promised him the whole thing would be kept quiet if he returned the bonds and the stock certificate immediately? If he refused to give them up, Jim O'Neill could be asked to have a talk with him. If that did no good, then, and not until then, the police would have to be called in.

He dialed Beecher's, got Dean on the wire, and told him he must see him at once at his apartment.

Dean said, "I'll be right over, Mr. Riggott." He knew from the other man's icy tone that it wasn't a social visit. The bubble had burst.

Three

The car Dean drove to Leonard's wasn't the 1946 Plymouth he had driven there eleven days ago. This one was a 1951 model he had bought only yesterday.

On the way to the apartment he settled his course of action. He would deny the theft; it was the only thing he could do.

Leonard greeted him coldly. He led him to the den, sat down, and in a flat voice made his accusation.

Dean showed indignation. "This is the most frightful thing I ever heard of," he declared. "I know nothing about your bonds or your Atlantic certificate. I can't imagine your making such a charge against me, Mr. Riggott. No one's ever called me a thief before."

He said much more in this vein. It was meant to be a convincing display of outraged innocence. But it made no impression on Leonard Riggott. When he could get in a word he said, "Dean, no matter what you say, I know you took those bonds. You—"

"I didn't take them! The only guilt I have is that I did go out of here and leave the door unlocked.

Some thief—"

Riggott's patience was wearing thin. He had expected protestations of innocence, but he had expected them to be accompanied by confusion and other marks of guilt. A confession would follow and then the offer to restore what was stolen. The last thing he expected was this unabashed claim of innocence maintained much too long.

"Let's not waste time talking about sneak thieves who miraculously hit on the combination of my safe, find the key, and make off with the bonds all within ten minutes," he snapped.

"I don't say they were taken that night. I say a thief got in, took an impression of the lock on the door, came back when you were out, and then got the safe open," Dean retorted coolly. "For that matter, the thief could have been getting in here and working on the safe long before I left the door open the other night."

Leonard drew a long breath and glowered at the young man. But he spoke quietly. "Dean, for Tad's sake, for your father's sake, too, I'm prepared to let this go without having you arrested. All I ask is that you return my property and then get out of Hampton. That's all. I consider it a very reasonable offer. Meet those two conditions and no one will ever hear from me what you've done." He paused before he added, "That's fair enough, isn't it?"

Dean took his time over his reply. For all his outer coolness, he was inwardly in a frenzy. Leonard's call had caught him unprepared. Nearly two weeks had gone by since his theft and he'd felt more and more sure of getting away with it. Now he was caught and should accept Riggott's offer.

But would the offer still hold when the other man heard he'd spent over fifteen hundred dollars of his money? It wasn't likely. If it did, at the very least he would demand that everything Dean had bought should be turned over to him to be sold for whatever it would bring.

Dean thought of the warm affection Elaine had shown toward him last week end in her delight over her ring and gold charm. Was he to tell her they were bought with stolen money and take them back? Never, he resolved to himself. No matter what.

He looked at Leonard and said with firmness, "I can't return what I haven't got. I didn't touch your bonds. I don't know what happened to them."

Even as he spoke, chilling images were flashing through his mind; the police, looking into his affairs, finding out about the car he'd bought yesterday—he never should have bought it so soon—and asking, "Where'd you get the money for this car, Lipscomb?" He could almost hear official voices pressing the question. Then the inquiry would broaden out to Elaine, the diamond he'd bought her—

There were no steps he wouldn't take to keep her from finding out what he had done.

Leonard said, "Dean, I'll tell you how I feel about this. Instead of rushing you on it, I'm going to give you every chance to think it over. Right now, while you're here, I'm going to call Jim O'Neill, the county detective. He's a neighbor of mine at High Point Lake and we're on pretty friendly terms. I'll ask him if he'll be at his office tomorrow morning and if I can see him there. If he says yes, I'll let you go home and give some thought to the tough spot you're in. You'll have until

35

tomorrow to bring those bonds—and the stock certificate—back to me."

As he was speaking, Leonard reached for the telephone directory, looked up the number of the state's attorney's office, and dialed it. When he was put through to the county detective he said, "Hello. Jim? . . . This is Len Riggott. How are you? . . . Good. And your wife and the children? . . . Good. Say, are you in your office on Saturday morning? . . . You will be tomorrow? Well, would you mind if I happened to drop in? . . . No, there's no hurry about it—in fact I may not need to talk to you at all. But if I do, I wanted to make sure you'd be in and could arrange to see me. Thanks a lot . . . Yes, I will. Good-by."

He hung up and looked at Dean. "There it is, right on the line," he said. "You have until tomorrow morning to return the bonds. I'll expect you to be here with them at ten o'clock. If you persist in saying you haven't got them, we'll go over to see Jim O'Neill and you can try that story on him." He stood up in dismissal and then, as Dean got to his feet, he added, "Don't get any ideas about running away. The police would catch up with you fast enough."

"I'll be here at ten tomorrow," the young man informed him. "I have no reason to run away."

Leonard looked him up and down. "You won't do it, not because you have no reason to but because of that wife of yours. From what I hear, she's not half as crazy about you as you are about her. I don't imagine she'd want to join you in the life of a fugitive."

Dean said nothing. The fury in his eyes answered for him. He could have strangled the older man then and there for what he had just said.

He turned and walked out of the room, out of the apartment, out of the building. He had until ten o'clock tomorrow morning. It was four o'clock now. He had eighteen hours between him and ruin.

He got in his car and sat there staring straight ahead, trying to discipline his thoughts, make a plan, find a way out.

He thought about Leonard Riggott, sure of recovering his bonds, sure Dean wouldn't run away, insultingly sure of this last. Because of Elaine. Elaine . . .

He mustn't think of her and the prospect of losing her for good. He must find a way out. . . .

He started his car. At first he drove without a destination, following streets that would take him out of the city. But somewhere along the way he reached a decision. It involved crossing the gulf that lay between being a young man of good middle-class background and weak character and becoming a murderer.

On the open road he drove slowly. The April sun was still high overhead and all around him spring was showing a froth of green. It was an incongruously beautiful afternoon for the kind of thought Dean nourished. Murder belonged to the night, to storms and high winds blowing, and old moons dim in the sky. But it wasn't at night, it was on this April afternoon that Dean mentally, emotionally, crossed the gulf and became in intent a murderer. All that remained to make him one in fact as well as intent was a plan.

He looked at his watch. It was six-thirty. He had fifteen and a half hours left.

He was conscious of hunger. He stopped at a roadside diner. But when he was seated in a booth with a menu in front of him, the thought of solid food repelled him. He ordered soup and coffee instead and sat looking out the window, lighting his pipe and developing a plan.

It was based on two premises: that he must kill Leonard before he had a chance to talk to Jim O'Neill; that he must kill him away from his apartment in order to cut down on the risk and in order to conceal the body.

At first he didn't see how he was to get around Leonard's expressed intention of calling on the county detective at ten the next morning. But then, beginning with the premise that if the latter was kept away from his office Leonard wouldn't be able to call on him there, Dean's plan took shape.

He didn't know where Jim O'Neill lived, but he did know he owned a summer place at High Point Lake.

His mind's eye located the low shingled cottage among the others in the little group that stood side by side along a strip of beach. There was Leonard's, the largest of all, built, Tad had said, forty years ago by Leonard's parents. It was an ark of a place with a veranda running around two sides of it and a flight of steps leading down to a dock. Next to it was the cottage Tad had pointed out as Jim O'Neill's. Beyond it was Tad's, then two more cottages. Surrounding them was a wood that ran down to the lake. A dirt road cut through the wood. It would not be in use at this time of the year.

There were no shutters on the O'Neill cottage, Dean remembered. It shouldn't be difficult to break in. . . .

The rest of the plan seemed to unfold itself of its own accord.

It was after twelve that night when the state police discovered that vandalism had taken place at Jim O'Neill's cottage. They waited until seven-thirty the next morning to let him know about it.

Jim was taking a shower when they called him. It was Margaret, his wife, not yet emerged from her early-morning comatose state, who answered the call and summoned him.

The upstairs phone was by their bed. Jim, wrapped in a towel, his bare feet leaving large wet tracks on the floor, his black hair with its streaks of gray standing on end, picked up the receiver, muttering that it was too bad people couldn't stay off the goddamn phone until a man got dressed and had his breakfast. He said, "Hello?" abruptly.

Margaret put on her robe and began to brush her hair, watching her husband in the mirror over the dresser. Even like this, scowling and unkempt, he was still, she reflected fondly, a good-looking man who was holding his years nicely, his big body showing no signs of slackness as he got on in his forties.

She saw his scowl deepen. "For God's sake," he said. Then, "Is it very bad?" Then, "I see. What about the other cottages? . . . Uh-huh. Well, thanks very much for calling. I'll get up there right away. . . . Yeah, I was going to my office, but it's not urgent. . . . Okay, I wish you would. Nine o'clock suit you? . . . All right, I'll see you then."

His face was grim as he hung up and turned to Margaret. "That was Lieutenant Schmidt from the Garfield Barracks. He says our cottage was broken into last night. He thinks it was done by teen-agers. They

39

took the place apart, he says, but it doesn't look as if they did much real damage. He wants me up there right away to see if anything's missing."

"Oh dear," Margaret exclaimed in dismay. "I'd better go with you. You wouldn't know if any of the linens and things had been taken." She pulled off her robe and started to dress. "I'll call Mrs. Oldfield and she'll take the children."

Jim, too, started to dress. He said, "Apparently ours was the only cottage that was broken into. Out of the five of them, it had to be ours."

Margaret, pulling on plaid wool slacks, said, "It's funny it was only ours. I'd expect a bunch of boys doing a thing like that to break into several places while they were at it."

"Schmidt said just ours," Jim told her. "He said, though, that he was going to call the others and tell them about it in case they wanted to check on their cottages."

"How'd the police find out about it? When did it happen?"

"Last night. Some man who was driving through called the barracks and said he'd just given a ride to three teen-age boys and that from the way they talked he thought they'd been up to something at the lake. He described where he'd picked them up—where our road comes out on the highway—and a man went out from the barracks to take a look around. That's how they found out about it." Jim picked up a comb and ran it through his hair. "Young bastards," he said. "I'd like to lay my hands on them. You get the kids dressed. I'll go down and start the coffee."

Half an hour later, after a hasty breakfast, Margaret sent eight-year-old Sarah and four-year-old Loria over to stay with the obliging Mrs. Oldfield, who lived next door, and Jim and she started for High Point Lake.

It wasn't a long drive. It was only twenty miles from Warrenton, where they lived, and Hampton, where Jim's office was located. Margaret had thought it a great advantage three years ago when they bought the cottage that it was so convenient to both places. It meant they could go there until late in the fall and start going again early in the spring; and when they went there to stay for the summer after school closed, it meant Jim had little farther to travel to his office than when they were in Warrenton.

There were many occasions, however, when they both felt that the lake was too conveniently located. Friends and acquaintances appeared in great numbers to go swimming.

At nine o'clock they were turning onto the dirt road that led to the lake. They found that Lieutenant Schmidt and a state trooper had already arrived and were waiting outside the cottage for them.

They went in together through the back door, where a pane of glass had been broken to reach inside and turn the lock.

The O'Neills' first impression was of chaos. Every cabinet and drawer in the kitchen had been opened and their contents strewn on the floor. In the living room books were thrown around, cushions pulled off the chairs, tables knocked over, ashes from the fireplace smeared on the rugs. In the bedrooms was the same wild disorder: drawers and closets emptied, clothing

41

and linens flung about, the bedding pulled off the beds, the curtains dragged down from the windows.

Jim became more and more profane as they moved from one room to another. But in the end, when they had looked at everything, Margaret and he agreed that except for a few broken dishes and the pane of glass in the back door, no real damage had been done and nothing seemed to have been stolen.

"It will take us the whole day to get the place straightened out," Margaret said. "But thank goodness it isn't any worse. I've heard horrifying tales of vandalism at summer cottages."

"There've been some right here at this lake," the lieutenant informed her. "You people had better get shutters and padlocks on before another winter."

"Don't worry, I will," Jim replied. "I've been going to do it ever since we bought the place. But that's the way it is. You lock the barn door after the horse is stolen."

"Not exactly stolen," Margaret said.

"All right." He smiled at her, his good humor restored all at once. "Kicked around, let's say."

He went outside with the other two men, who were preparing to leave. Lieutenant Schmidt said they had already started to question some of the boys in the vicinity who had been in trouble before; he hoped he'd get hold of the right ones very soon. "Too bad," he added, "that guy who called in didn't stick around or at least give us his name. We might have got descriptions of them that would help."

"Maybe," Jim said. "At least, as long as there was only one witness, you'd have only one set of descriptions."

42

The lieutenant laughed. "That's right. One witness, one set of descriptions. Two witnesses, two sets. And so on."

He opened the door of the police car. The trooper was behind the wheel. "I'll keep in touch with you," he said. "Awfully sorry it happened. Right in my back yard, too."

"My own fault," Jim told him. "I should have had the place shut up tighter."

As they drove away he turned back to the cottage. He felt better, relieved that the damage wasn't more serious and that none of the nasty little acts of perversion that sometimes accompanied this type of vandalism had been committed. Margaret had been spared that much.

The unknown motorist who had called the state police occupied no place in his thoughts. The man's behavior seemed natural enough. He was from out of state, he'd said, just driving through and hadn't wanted to get involved in anything. And when he called he'd been acting only on suspicion; for all he knew, the boys he'd picked up could have been indulging in idle talk.

Tad and Phoebe Beecher arrived a few minutes later. Lieutenant Schmidt had called them, they said, and they'd come out to make sure their own cottage was all right and to offer their help to the O'Neills.

The Saxtons, Glenn and Nicky and their three-year-old son, were the next to appear. Toward noon Loretta Madler arrived. All the colony was now present except for Leonard Riggott.

His nephew Glenn accounted for him. "He called me after he'd heard from the state police," Glenn said. "He didn't know whether or not he'd be able to get out here today. I have a key to his cottage and he told me if he didn't get here by noon I was to go in and take a look around."

Leonard didn't appear by noon. While Tad and Jim drove to the village to buy sandwiches and coffee and a pane of glass for the back door—everyone had stayed to help and by this time the cottage was almost back in order—Glenn went next door to his uncle's on a tour of inspection.

He returned to say that Leonard's cottage had not been entered. He had looked through every room and had found nothing wrong.

There was general agreement that it was a shame the O'Neills had had all the bad luck, but that even so, what had happened at their place could have been worse.

By two o'clock the cleaning-up party was over and everyone went home.

When Glenn got back to Hampton he tried to phone his uncle to tell him no damage had been done at his cottage. There was no answer. He tried again the next day and the next. Finally, he called the superintendent, who said, "I haven't seen Mr. Riggott around the last two or three days. He was going away, wasn't he?"

"Yes, he was. But I expected him to call me before he left."

"Maybe he was in a hurry and it slipped his mind."

"Maybe that was it." Glenn thanked the superintendent and hung up, feeling a little injured. His uncle should have called to say good-by, no matter how rushed he was.

He told Nicky about it. She said, "Well, perhaps he did call and we weren't here."

"But his cottage—"

"He knew it was all right. The police told him it was. Don't fuss about it. When he gets around to it he'll let you hear from him."

Nicky was right, Glenn thought. He dropped the subject and made no further efforts to get in touch with his uncle.

Four

Leonard Riggott was still in bed that Saturday morning when he received his call from Lieutenant Schmidt about the vandalism at the lake the night before, but his sleepiness vanished as soon as he heard what the police officer had to say.

"You're sure my cottage seems to be all right?" He kept pressing the point. It was his cottage, one of his possessions. He expressed only perfunctory concern over what had happened at the O'Neills'. Then he asked, "Is O'Neill going up there this morning?"

"Yes, I'm to meet him at nine o'clock."

"Will he be there all day?" Leonard's thoughts were moving ahead to what he should do if Dean still proved recalcitrant and Jim wasn't available.

"I imagine so. He'll be busy getting his place straightened out."

"Well . . . I'll try to get up there myself sometime today—although you do feel sure my cottage wasn't broken into?"

"It shows no signs of it," Schmidt replied patiently.

"Well, then, thanks for calling, Lieutenant."

"You're welcome." Schmidt, as he hung up, thought, "What a pest he is," and dismissed Leonard from his mind.

The latter immediately dialed Glenn Saxton's number and made his request that his nephew inspect his cottage if he himself hadn't appeared at the lake by noon. Then he dressed and had breakfast at the coffee shop downstairs.

At five minutes of ten he was back in his apartment, pacing the living room while he waited for Dean. He couldn't decide what his next step should be if the young man persisted in denying he had the bonds. He had counted on taking the problem to Jim O'Neill. It was most inconvenient, he reflected, that today of all days the county detective should have been called away.

He felt less inclined than ever to go to the police. The very thought of it was too unpleasant to contemplate.

He told himself that perhaps all his worrying was needless; perhaps Dean, having had time to consider his position, knew he had no chance of getting away with what he had done.

Leonard glanced at his watch. It was just ten o'clock. Dean should be here any moment to bring back what he had stolen. Then Leonard would tell him to get out of Hampton and the whole disagreeable affair would be ended. No one but themselves would ever know about it. . . .

Two or three minutes later Dean arrived without the bonds.

"I couldn't bring what I haven't got," he said. "I've been hoping that when you calmed down and thought

47

it over you'd withdraw this fantastic accusation you've made."

Leonard looked at him and trembled with anger at his intransigence, the brazenness of his attitude. He walked away from him, trying to compose himself. It would have to be the police after all, he thought. There was no help for it.

He hadn't asked Dean to sit down. The latter stood near the foyer, his gaze fixed on the other man, who had the power to bring him to ruin. He said, "Mr. Riggott, I'm perfectly willing to go to the county detective with you and tell him what I've told you."

"He's not at his office today," Leonard informed him curtly. "He's at his place at the lake. It was broken into last night."

This was the moment toward which all Dean's efforts had been directed. He tried to strike a casual note as he said, "Well, then, why don't we go to the lake and see him?"

"He'll have other things on his mind. He won't have time to talk to us."

"You said he was a friend of yours. He ought to be able to spare a few minutes for an important thing like this."

Leonard made no immediate reply. He was thinking about Dean's proposal, and the more he thought about it the better it looked to him. It resolved his quandary; it meant he needn't go to the police at once.

He said, "All right, if that's the way you want it, that's the way we'll do it."

There was one more hurdle to get over, the use of Dean's car rather then Leonard's, which would have complicated the situation later on for Dean. But even that went off smoothly. Outside the building the older man hesitated and said, "My car's in the garage around the corner," but when Dean replied, "Let's use mine, it's right here," he made no protest.

He didn't know it had been bought only two days ago with his money. He had never seen Dean's other car.

They headed for the lake, prospective murderer and prospective victim. Leonard wouldn't, of course, have been there if he'd had a glimmer of suspicion that these were the roles Dean had assigned them. He thought of the latter as a young scoundrel; but he also thought of him as his father's son and Tad's protégé, not as a desperate figure whose company spelled mortal danger to him. From time to time he glanced at Dean and thought, "Jim will know how to handle him. He'll break him down."

There was little conversation between them during the drive. Twice Leonard tried to persuade him of the folly of his stand. Both times Dean reiterated his innocence. Then Leonard lapsed into bitter, frustrated silence.

The younger man's silence was of a different kind, filled with determination. He was going to kill Leonard.

He knew where he was going to do it. Last night, driving around in the area of the lake, he had picked the place. He had an ample choice of lonely countryside solidly wooded on both sides of the highway with occasional dirt roads branching off into the woods. Garfield village lay beyond the lake; as one approached it from the Hampton side there were no houses to be seen for a long stretch.

It was along this stretch that Dean swung his car into one of the dirt roads, bringing from Leonard the startled protest, "Hey, this isn't the right road! We've got almost two miles to go yet."

"What? Are you sure? There was a big tree where I turned in. I remember noticing it when I went to the lake with the Beechers."

"I don't care what you noticed, this isn't the right road. I ought to know, all the years I've been going to the lake."

Dean was driving deeper and deeper into the wood while this exchange was taking place. Already the highway was out of sight.

"I'm sorry," he said. "I thought it was the right road. Won't it bring us out at the lake eventually?"

"No, it won't. It doesn't go anywhere. It comes to an end a couple of miles ahead."

"Well, I'll have to find a place to turn around." Dean's eyes were on the speedometer. They were now half a mile in from the highway. Another half mile and then—

"Can't you back out?" the older man demanded. He scanned the road in front of them. "I don't see any place where you can turn around."

"Too far to back out. Don't worry, I'll find a place."

"If you'd stopped when I told you it was the wrong road, you could have backed out with no trouble at all," Leonard reminded him. His voice was sharp with annoyance, but there was neither fear nor suspicion in it. He looked straight ahead, watching for an open space where the car could be turned around.

The road became poorer and narrower. Dean eyed the speedometer again. They were more than a mile in from the highway. He need go no farther.

He braked the car to a stop in a place where there was a little open ground on each side. He didn't look at Leonard as he said, "I think I can make it here if you don't mind getting out to direct me."

Sour impatience revealed itself on the other man's face, but he said nothing. He got out of the car and began to give directions for turning around.

Dean followed them, deathly pale, not looking at Leonard even once as he backed and turned, swinging the wheel to the right or the left according to what Leonard, standing off to the rear, said.

There was just a moment after the car was faced around toward the highway when Dean's nerve failed. He felt as if he couldn't go on with it. Then, reminding himself of what would happen if he didn't, he took out his gun, the .22 he had bought years ago for target shooting.

Leonard was moving toward him with the intention of getting back in the car. He was about three feet away when Dean stepped out of it with the gun pointed at him.

He came to a dead stop, the blood draining from his face, a look of realization and terror spreading across it. As he opened his mouth to scream Dean released the safety catch and fired. Leonard was dead before he struck the ground.

Dean stood where he was, looking down at the dead man. He returned the gun to his pocket. The echoes of the shot died away. It became possible to listen for footsteps running toward him, voices calling, "What happened? What's going on here?"

But the quiet remained unbroken. The first sound he

could distinguish was the slight rustle of new leaves overhead and presently, as his hearing sharpened, other small sounds of the woods.

Dean had thought he couldn't move. But all at once he became frantic to get away. He hurried around in back of his car and opened the trunk to take out the khaki wool blanket he had bought that morning. He spread it out on the ground beside the body, which he rolled over on it face upward. There was no blood visible. He pulled back the topcoat and suit jacket and saw a little of it seeping through the shirt. He felt a squeamish hesitancy about going through the dead man's pockets, but he had to have his keys. He found them and put them in his own pocket. His haste took on a fevered quality as he wrapped the body in the blanket, got it up on his shoulder, and put it in the trunk of the car. Leonard's hat had fallen off. He picked it up, threw it in on top of the body, and closed the trunk, slamming it to make certain it was locked.

He drove back to the highway. There was no one in sight when he reached it, no one to mark his emergence from the wood where he had killed a man.

Dean drove back to Hampton without incident. He drove with the greatest care; he mustn't become involved in an accident while he had Leonard's body in the trunk of his car.

He parked in his allotted space in the yard of his rooming house and climbed the stairs to his room. He felt completely exhausted. He lay down on the bed and fell into a stupefied sleep that lasted until nightfall.

That night and the next day Dean ate his meals at a restaurant within walking distance of the rooming house. He didn't take his car out of the yard until he

52

went to work Monday morning.

At five o'clock in the afternoon he left Beecher's and drove to the lake. Tad had told him what had happened there and that the state police were going to keep a closer eye on the little colony. So far, Tad said, they hadn't got hold of the boys who had broken into the O'Neill cottage, but they were working hard on it.

Dean reasoned that it was safe enough to go there in broad daylight. The police car wouldn't be around looking for vandals until after dark.

Nevertheless, he took precautions, coming to a stop before he rounded the last bend, which would bring the colony into view, and going ahead on foot through the wood to make a preliminary survey.

The five cottages, standing in a row, showed no signs of occupancy and no cars were parked outside them. But Dean was startled to see how many boats there were out on the lake. Within his range of vision he counted four. They were far out from the shore, but still they were there. They were fishermen. He remembered Tad's having said the fishing season had opened.

They couldn't be helped, there was nothing he could do about them. He had to go ahead with his plan for disposing of Leonard's body. As fast as he could he'd get away from there.

He went back to his car and drove it to the door of the garage built under Leonard's cottage. One of the keys in the dead man's key case fitted the padlock. Dean drove into the garage, closed the door, and went up an inner flight of steps that led into the kitchen.

He made a swift tour of the first floor, where there were four big rooms and a lavatory, and went upstairs.

Here there were four bedrooms and two bathrooms. There were large halls upstairs and down. The cottage had been built by Leonard Riggott's parents in an era when spaciousness was in demand.

Dean had no trouble identifying the dead man's bedroom. It was at the front overlooking the lake with a private bathroom opening off it and various personal belongings in evidence. This was where Dean intended to leave the body.

Getting it out of the trunk and carrying it up to the bedroom was a grim affair. He had to fight a feeling of sickness and make stops to rest and catch his breath.

At last he had it in the room. He laid it down near the door while he pulled the bed apart, kicked up the rugs, knocked over chairs, and threw a lamp on the floor. He hoped that when the body was found the police would assume it was here, after a struggle, that Leonard had been killed and, with his watch and wallet missing, that robbery had been the motive. It would be their business to try to figure out what Leonard had been doing at his cottage without his car.

The body was in a half crouch after its two days in the trunk of Dean's car. He placed it against the side of the bed. His eyes avoided the dead face, but even through the gloves he wore there was no avoiding the feel of the dead flesh as he removed the wrist watch and wallet and spread the fingers out on the disordered bedclothes to make it look as if Leonard had been clutching at them as he died.

He picked up the blanket and stood in the doorway surveying his work. It looked authentic to him. He hadn't taken off Leonard's topcoat because the bullet had gone through it and it had soaked up what little blood there had been. The police must infer that he had just arrived at the cottage when he had been attacked by his murderer. His hat had better be in the room.

He went down to get it and left the blanket on the seat of his car. He would drop it somewhere in the woods on his way home. It couldn't be traced to him.

He carried the hat upstairs and placed it on a chest, Leonard's key case beside it. The back door was self-locking and he would snap the padlock on the garage door to lock that.

He stood back and once more his glance went around the room. The shutters on all the windows were closed and he had opened the slats on the front ones to give him light while he worked. The sun slanted through them and picked out his footprints in the dust on the floor. Dean caught his breath. It was lucky he'd noticed them. He'd read somewhere that the police made casts of footprints.

He hunted out a dust mop and dusted the bedroom and hall floors and every other wood or linoleum surface on which he'd walked.

That took care of everything, he thought. Now, if the coast was clear outside, he was ready to leave. He peered out through the shutters at the back of the house and on both sides without seeing anyone. But when he went in the living room and looked out from there, he saw a fisherman in a rowboat dropping anchor a short distance away from Leonard's dock. While Dean watched, the fisherman made a cast and settled back with the air of a man prepared to stay indefinitely.

He stayed for two hours. He caught three fish. Dean, his eyes glued to the slat in the blind, kept count of them, alternately cursing the fisherman and imploring him to leave, wild with anxiety over this break in the clockwork precision with which his plans had gone forward until now.

At sunset the man was still there. Daylight Time had come in over the weekend and the light held until after eight o'clock. Inside the cottage with its closed shutters night fell much earlier. Dean could no longer try to quiet his nerves by intervals of walking the floor. It was too dark to see where he was going in the unfamiliar room.

He sat down by the window again. It gave him something to do to take out his pipe and penknife and scrape the dottle from the pipe into an envelope he found in his pocket. He folded the envelope and put it back where he had found it, moving away from the window to fill and light his pipe.

Dean was still toying with the penknife when he resumed his vigil at the blind. He drew the point of the knife back and forth across the window sill, his whole being concentrated on the man in the boat.

In the few minutes he had been away from the window the light outside had faded noticeably. He felt panicky. What should he do? Take a chance and leave? Would the man pay any attention to him if he did? What about the state police? How soon after dark would they begin to check on the cottages?

Dean couldn't make up his mind what to do. He sat with his face pressed against the slats of the shutter turning the penknife over and over in his hands. They felt hot and sweaty. He took off his gloves and put them on again. He looked out through the blind, blinking at what he saw, not daring to believe it was happening at last. The fisherman was pulling up his anchor. A moment later he rowed away.

Dean forced himself to stay where he was a few minutes longer until he lost sight of the boat in the dusk. Then he sprang to his feet, and stumbling and groping through the darkness he made his way to the garage.

He needed his headlights but he didn't turn them on. He backed the car out, snapped the padlock shut on the garage door, and drove off, holding his breath in fear of meeting a police car on the lake road. He didn't turn on his lights until he swung out on the highway, free at last, safe at last.

that one about him," Phoebe suggested.

Margaret mentally shook her head over Phoebe's

Five

The day after school closed in June the O'Neills
moved out to the lake for the summer. They were the
last members of the colony to arrive. The others, who
had no children or none of school age, had established
themselves weeks earlier.

Sunday was cool and cloudy that week end and the
O'Neills had no visitors. They worked around the
cottage all day and in the evening the Saxtons and
Beechers dropped in.

The three men grouped themselves at one end of the
living room, the three women at the other. Nicky
Saxton lost no time in reporting that Loretta Madler
had a new beau. "A friend of mine saw them having
dinner together twice last week," she said. "I wonder
why she hasn't brought him out here."

Margaret and Phoebe Beecher were immediately
interested. Last summer Loretta's pursuit of Leonard
Riggott had furnished them with a topic of conversation that never palled.

"Maybe she doesn't want to for fear your uncle will

find out about him," Phoebe suggested.

Margaret mentally shook her head over Phoebe's naïveté. How could the latter have forgotten so completely the tactics employed in getting your man?

"That can't be it," she said. "She'd want to show him off if she could and have it get back to Len that he had some competition."

"I was thinking maybe he's a married man and one of us might know him," Nicky offered.

"That might be it," Margaret agreed.

"Uncle Len wouldn't care how many men she had," Nicky continued. "He gave her the air before he went away. For good."

"Really?" Margaret and Phoebe exclaimed in unison. "You're sure?"

"Yes, I'm sure." Nicky, with a qualm of uneasiness, glanced at her husband who was at the other end of the room. Glenn wouldn't like her talking about his uncle's affairs this way. She added hastily, "But please don't mention it to anyone."

"Oh, we won't," Margaret and Phoebe assured her.

"I felt all along she wouldn't land him," Margaret said next. "A hardened bachelor like him, she ought to have known it herself."

"And the way she threw herself at him," Nicky said.

"Not a bit clever of her," Margaret said.

"Indeed not," Phoebe said.

They fell silent, each of them thinking of her own success in marrying the man of her choice and neglecting to remember the tribulations that had preceded her triumphant arrival at the altar.

Margaret broke the silence by asking Nicky, "Have you heard from your uncle lately?"

"Lately? Why, we haven't heard at all since he went away the end of April. He never writes very often, but by this time we should at least have had a card from him. As Glenn says, suppose something came up that needed his attention? We know he went to Vancouver first, but we have no idea of where he is now. He really ought to let us hear from him."

Margaret and Phoebe said it wasn't very thoughtful of Leonard not to have written. Then the conversation moved on to something else.

In general, Margaret was scrupulous about not betraying confidences, but whenever she promised she wouldn't, she made a mental exception of Jim. He was her husband. She felt justified in telling him whatever she pleased.

That night, then, at bedtime, she regarded herself as free to tell him about Leonard's having broken off with Loretta.

"He's well out of it," Jim commented. "She's a pain in the neck."

That was all he would say about it. Men were unpredictable when it came to gossip, Margaret reflected while she was getting undressed. Sometimes they entered into it; other times, like Jim tonight, they just weren't interested.

In spite of this reflection, she went on to inform her husband that Leonard hadn't written to his nephew since he went away in April.

"I never write letters either if I can help it," Jim said.

"Yes, but he's been gone almost two months. Something urgent might have come up that they needed to get hold of him."

"Well, it hasn't," was Jim's reply. He got into bed

and pulled up the blanket at the foot of it. "Cold tonight," he said. "I don't think you should let the kids go in the water tomorrow unless it gets a lot warmer."

"I won't," Margaret answered, keeping to herself the thought that the admonition was quite unnecessary.

By the time she put out the light and got into bed Jim was already beginning to doze. She edged her icy feet over against his and it brought only a grunt from him. Within another minute or two he was fast asleep.

Margaret was wakeful. Her thoughts went from Leonard's jilting of Loretta to his carelessness in not writing to Glenn. How did he know all this time that something hadn't happened to Glenn, his only close relative, or to Nicky, or to Tommy, their son? It wasn't right that he didn't keep Glenn informed of his whereabouts.

But it was the kind of behavior you could expect from Leonard Riggott, she thought next. No matter how friendly he seemed on the surface, he was a cold, self-centered man.

Her thoughts moved on to what Phoebe had said about Tad and her flying out to Denver Tuesday to attend the wedding of his niece. They'd be gone about a week, she'd said, and while they were away Dean Lipscomb and his wife were going to come out from town and stay at the Beecher cottage.

"That furnished apartment of theirs is in what used to be the attic of an old house," Phoebe had added, "and it's frightfully hot, Elaine says. It will be a nice change for them to be out here. In fact, I was telling Tad tonight it wouldn't hurt us to invite them to stay on for a week or two after we get back. We have plenty of room and Dean could drive back and forth to

Hampton every day like the rest of the men do. It would be good for Elaine to have company during the day. It's lonely for her in Hampton. She doesn't know many people yet."

Margaret hoped Phoebe would reconsider issuing an invitation to the Lipscombs to stay on at the lake. The group was so small that it would mean a closer association with Elaine than Margaret wanted to have. She had met her two or three times and had been disturbed by her indifferent attitude toward Dean who was so obviously devoted to his wife.

Margaret had liked Dean better, but she thought he lacked backbone. He let Elaine make the decisions, he was under her thumb. A man should be the head of his own house, the way Jim was the head of his—or rather, she corrected herself with all honesty—the way Jim and the rest of the world thought he was. Whenever she did arrange things to go as she felt they should, she at least kept hidden the devices she employed. Jim wouldn't accept for a moment the kind of treatment Elaine accorded her husband. Jim had too much self-respect.

Margaret put out her hand and touched his broad back. She moved closer to him. She was smiling a little as she went to sleep.

Monday was warm and sunny. In the morning Margaret did such housework as seemed necessary and drove to Garfield village for groceries. In the afternoon she went swimming and lazed on the beach. That was her day.

Jim's day at his office in Hampton ended on an unpleasant note with a visit from a state legislator with important connections at the capitol. He came on behalf of a friend who was under indictment for shady practices in municipal affairs. He wanted the indictment squashed.

Jim heard him out and said he would call the matter to Goodrich's attention, but that he doubted it would do much good.

The legislator went on insisting that his friend was a man of the highest integrity, the victim of a set of circumstances that looked bad but really weren't. There must be something that Goodrich, the state's attorney, could do to help him.

The grand jury, viewing the friend in a different light, had returned an indictment that accused him of dipping his hand in the public till. Jim reminded the legislator that the state's attorney had to act on such an indictment. It could not be squashed.

When the legislator finally left he was in a bad humor.

"A bastard," Jim thought, showing him to the door. "I don't know why I have to have his kind in my hair every so often."

He was glad to clear his desk and leave for the lake.

Margaret was getting dinner when he arrived home. He kissed her and said dinner smelled good.

"Roast beef and those garlicky roast potatoes you like," she told him. "And strawberry shortcake for dessert. No whipped cream on it, though. Loria decided Juney and Rex were thirsty, so she poured what she thought was milk in their dishes. Only it wasn't milk, it was the half pint of cream I had for the shortcake. Juney and Rex lapped up every drop of it."

Jim laughed. "I hope you showed her the difference between milk and cream bottles."

"I did indeed."

He went into their bedroom, took off his holster, and removed the bullets from his gun, dropping them in his pocket. He hung the holster and gun in the closet. This was his nightly custom on reaching home, a safety measure he had instituted when he first became a father.

"Where're the kids now?" he asked, when he returned to the kitchen. Even as he asked, he heard them. They had spied his car and came running from the wood. Mingled with their voices was the barking of Rex, the beagle puppy, a recent addition to the family, who adored the children and tried to conceal his fear of Juney, the tomcat, who had been a member of the household for three years. Sarah, only five when it was given to her, had named the cat June. She hadn't cared that the cat was male. She liked the name June, she said.

They called it Juney, which could mean, Margaret had pointed out to Jim, that its name was Junius or Juniper or anything less flagrantly feminine than June.

"Daddy! Daddy!" Sarah and Loria burst into the kitchen and flung themselves at Jim with as much enthusiasm as if they had been parted from him for years rather than hours, while Rex, sharing it, tried to climb his legs.

Sarah was carrying a pail. She dropped it on the floor before she flung herself at her father and water splashed in all directions. "Daddy, I've got wonderful news for you!" she cried. "I caught four more tadpoles in the brook. Look, they're in the pail."

"I helped catch them," Loria declared, swinging back and forth on Jim's arm.

"You did not."

"I did so."

"Loria, how can you say that?" Sarah's hazel eyes, which were like Jim's, were turned on her four-year-old sister with a look designed to wither. "All you did was make a lot of splashes that scared them away."

"I helped catch them," Loria maintained imperturbably.

"Well, let's look at them." Jim bent over the pail. "Doesn't matter who caught them as long as they're caught—there's only three. I thought you said there were four."

"There are four." Sarah and Loria knelt beside the pail counting. The count wouldn't come out four. One of the tadpoles had vanished during the dash from the wood to the cottage to greet Jim. The children raced out the back door to look for it, Rex at their heels.

Margaret and Jim looked at each other and laughed. He carried the pail out on the back porch while she mopped up the water that had spilled out of it.

"That old washtub isn't going to hold many more frogs and tadpoles and turtles," she remarked. "We'll have to get another one."

"Too bad they don't eat each other," Jim said, as he came back in the kitchen. "That would help to keep the population down. You'd think Juney would help, too, by dipping in a paw now and then. You wouldn't expect the screen they've got over the tub to stop him."

Juney, who was a large black and white cat, was lying on the window sill. He turned his head languidly at the sound of his name and began to wash a paw already snowy.

Margaret glanced at him. "No," she said, "I don't

imagine that's it. I don't think Juney would deign to dirty one of his beautiful paws in that slimy old washtub. Why should he? He eats regularly without going to that much trouble. He doesn't like raw fish anyway."

"You got a point," Jim agreed.

That evening, after Margaret had put the children to bed, the Beechers came over to say good-by. They were leaving for Denver in the morning. Dean and Elaine, who had come out that day to stay at the lake, accompanied the older couple.

While Jim mixed drinks for everyone, Tad trailing him out to the kitchen, Margaret sat on the porch with the others: Phoebe, comfortably stout, easygoing; Elaine, slender, blond, with a full sulky mouth and cool gray eyes; Dean, good-looking, boyish, watching his wife, always, Margaret thought, with a shadow of anxiety in his eyes.

Loretta Madler came up the porch steps, the length of her legs accentuated by the shorts she wore. They were handsome legs already deeply tanned. She was a handsome woman built on a large scale. When the other three women in the group speculated about her age their estimates varied between thirty-five and forty-five. Phoebe, who was herself in her early fifties, said forty-five. Loretta's blue-black hair didn't show a thread of gray, but Phoebe gave the credit for that to her hairdresser.

"Hi, everybody," Loretta greeted them. "Margaret, I haven't a thing to read. Can I borrow something?"

"Couple of quarter mysteries suit you? I've read them both, so you needn't return them."

"Won't Jim want them?"

"No. He used to read one occasionally, but he's given it up. Too many dead blondes, he says. Sit down and have a drink with us."

Loretta sat down. Margaret went out to tell her husband to make an extra one.

Tad and Jim brought out the drinks. The talk turned to the Beechers' trip. Then Jim began to tell Dean about the good fishing the lake afforded, the rainbow and brown trout, the small- and large-mouth bass. Tad joined in and they talked about it at some length, although Margaret could see that Dean wasn't interested in fishing and that Elaine looked as if everything about the gathering bored her. But Jim and Tad were fishermen; there was no stopping them once they were started.

It was Loretta who finally managed to change the subject. "Has anyone heard from Len since he went to Vancouver?" she asked. Her manner was casual, but Margaret had been noticing how often her gaze strayed to the closed-up cottage next door.

"She's dying for some news of him," Margaret thought, her dark blue eyes resting sympathetically on the other woman. "She hasn't given up hope that she'll get him back. It's too bad."

Everyone said they hadn't heard from Leonard. Jim added, "Pretty nice, the way he can come and go as he pleases. No responsibilities like most of us have." But as he spoke he sent his wife a smile that told her he wouldn't change places with Leonard or anyone else.

"Who is this Len?" Elaine inquired.

Phoebe told her about him. Dean, silent in his chair, saw Elaine's eyes light with interest when she heard Leonard described as a wealthy foot-loose bachelor.

67

Dean's twinge of jealousy was automatic; it came before he remembered that there was no need for jealousy of Leonard Riggott.

The group broke up soon thereafter. The Beechers were leaving very early the next morning and Dean was to drive them to the airport.

When the others were gone Margaret went outside to take down her forgotten washing. There were lights shining in all the cottages except Leonard's. His was in darkness, somehow a forbidding outline in the dusk. The lake washing against his dock had a lonely sound.

"I wish he'd sell his place," she thought. "I wish he'd sell it to someone with two daughters the same age as Sarah and Loria."

From Margaret's point of view the one drawback to their cottage was the lack of children in the immediate vicinity for Sarah and Loria to play with.

Jim drifted out and began to help her take down the clothes. Margaret's thoughts took a new turn. "Loretta's still hoping she'll get Len back," she told him.

"Won't do her much good," he observed. "Once a man's through with a woman he's through with her."

His wife considered this statement. It was true. It was the way men were made. "Women are different," she said. "They're always taking men back after saying they won't."

"That's because women don't know what they want."

"Elaine Lipscomb does," Margaret averred.

"Does she? What?"

"Her own way in everything."

"Well, don't we all?"

68

"Jim, you know what I mean."

He grinned at her. "Sure I do. You mean she's right out in the open about it. Most of us beat around the bush. You, for instance. You're a great little bush beater."

Margaret gave him a quick glance. His expression was unreadable in the dimness. She decided not to challenge his remark. Why give him a chance to tell her outright that he saw through at least some of her roundabout methods of directing their affairs toward the ends she thought best for them?

Her methods were not roundabout enough, it seemed. They must have been furnishing him with inner amusement upon occasion. . . .

Men were the strangest creatures, she reflected with chagrin, as she took down the last piece of washing on the line. She'd been married to Jim for ten years, but still he could sometimes surprise her.

She consoled herself with the thought that she had grown so used to his occupation she tended to disregard it. But he was, after all, a detective. He'd acquired a backlog of understanding of people and their behavior.

He picked up the basket of clothes. "You're not going to iron tonight, are you?" he inquired. "I thought you might come down and sit on the dock with me while I throw out a line."

Margaret had intended to do some of the ironing, but she said, "No, I'm not going to. I'll go down on the dock with you."

She held open the screen door while he carried the clothes-basket into the kitchen. With seeming irrelevance, she remarked, "One of the things that's wrong with the Lipscombs' marriage is that Dean tries too hard to please Elaine. If he didn't try so hard, she might do a little of it."

Jim set down the basket. His hazel eyes twinkled as he looked at her. "I'll pass on my formula to him: Keep your wife happy by never trying to please her."

Margaret smiled. "It wouldn't do any good. Nothing would. She's a plain stinker, that's all. Dean is nice, though. A weak character but nice."

"You certainly form opinions of people on short acquaintance."

"Feminine intuition. I'm always guided by it in judging them. It's practically infallible."

"Oh." Jim raised a heavy dark eyebrow at her. "I could use you in my office."

He got out fishing tackle and they went down on the dock. The Lipscombs didn't come into their conversation again that evening, nor did they mention Leonard Riggott. But from time to time Margaret glanced at the dark bulk of the cottage next door, still wishing that its owner, who used it so little, would sell it to some congenial couple with two daughters aged eight and four.

Six

The following Monday Tad Beecher, back from Denver, settled down in his office with his partner to be brought up to date on the affairs of Beecher and Company. Almost immediately he received an unpleasant shock. His partner, in summarizing the buying and selling that had gone on during his absence, said, "We bought two hundred shares of Amalgamated Chemical for Riggott. It went below ninety Friday and I had your notation to pick up two hundred shares for him if it did go below that figure. We got it at eighty-nine. I tried to call him about it Friday, but I didn't catch him in. I'll call him this morning."

"Oh, for God's sake," Tad exclaimed. "I should have told you—I've been meaning to—that he isn't back from his trip and nobody seems to know where to get in touch with him since he went away. But we'll sure have to find out now."

He reached for the telephone directory, looked up the number of Glenn Saxton's advertising agency, and dialed it. When he was connected with Glenn he said,

"Hello. Tad Beecher calling. . . . Yes, yes, a fine time. Got home eleven-thirty last night. . . . Yes, indeed. Say, have you heard from your uncle yet? . . . You haven't? Well, that kind of leaves me out on a limb." He told Glenn about the stock purchase made in Leonard Riggott's name, concluding with, "So you see, I'll have to get in touch with him right away. If you'll give me the name and address of that friend in Vancouver, I'll take it from there."

He waited while Glenn looked up the address, wrote it down, thanked him, and hung up. In the meantime his partner had gone over to the board where the board boy was chalking up market quotations. He came back to Tad and announced glumly, "Amalgamated's down to eighty-seven."

Tad gave thought to what he should do. Ordinarily, Leonard was supposed to have his check in to pay for the two hundred shares of stock within five days of the purchase date. They could, of course, ask New York for an extension of another seven days. . . .

If they couldn't locate Leonard, he could only blame himself for the loss the firm would take. He should have told his partner what the situation was. But he just hadn't thought of it. Amalgamated had seemed to be fixed permanently at one hundred, and it was all of two months ago that Leonard had placed the conditional order.

Dean Lipscomb, though, had heard them talking at the lake about Leonard's not keeping his nephew posted on his whereabouts. If he'd only mentioned it to Tad's partner, the latter wouldn't have bought the stock—

No use thinking of that, Tad told himself. It was

nobody's fault but his. . . .

He wrote a telegram to Arthur Waite in Vancouver stating his need to get in touch with Leonard at once, asking for his present address, and adding reply collect to his message. He telephoned it in to Western Union and was informed by the girl on the desk that there was a good chance he would receive a reply before the day was over.

It came late in the afternoon. He was so taken aback by it that he had the girl repeat it twice. It ran, "Riggott never here. Have not heard from him since middle of April. Have no knowledge of his present address."

Tad picked up the phone and called Glenn. When he told him what he had learned the younger man said, "Well, I'll be damned." Then, "We'll have to do something about it."

"We certainly will." Tad was emphatic in agreement.

After an interval devoted to thought Glenn said, "I guess I'd better put in a call to Mr. Waite and find out how definite his arrangements with Uncle Len were supposed to have been, and so on." He paused. "Do you realize what this means? No one—so far as we know—has heard from Uncle Len or had any contact with him for two months. It's as if he vanished into thin air."

"That's right," Tad replied soberly. "You'd better call Waite this minute."

"I'll put the call right in. It may take time, though. If I don't call you back before you're ready to leave, I'll tell you about it tonight."

"Okay," Tad said. "You get to work on it."

Glenn hadn't called him by five o'clock. Tad left and started for the lake. Driving there, he thought about

73

Leonard with a sense of uneasiness that had its roots in their long acquaintance rather than in the possible financial loss his firm might take through the stock purchase.

It was a hell of a queer thing, he kept telling himself. A hell of a queer thing.

By the time Jim O'Neill arrived home, half an hour later than Tad, everyone in the colony knew that Leonard was missing. Margaret had just begun to tell her husband about it when Tad appeared to tell the story himself.

While he was telling it, Glenn drove into the yard. Nicky followed him to the O'Neills'.

"Waite couldn't tell me anything," Glenn said. "He had just one letter from Uncle Len, the middle of April, saying he'd start for Vancouver in about ten days and he'd send him a wire when he left. When Waite didn't hear anything more from him he sent him an air-mail letter to which he got no reply. Then he felt a little annoyed, he said, and he went off on a fishing trip with someone else. He hasn't heard a word from Uncle Len since." Glenn hesitated, glancing at Jim. "He thinks I should immediately take steps to find Uncle Len."

They were on the O'Neill back porch. Jim, who was leaning against the railing, said, "You will have to, of course."

Glenn made an uncertain gesture. "I don't know where to start."

The county detective was slow to reply. There was no way to tell yet how serious the situation was. If, he reflected, Riggott was away on some venture he wanted to keep private, he wouldn't thank his nephew for bringing the police in on it. It would be just as well to hold off on them—officially at least—until Glenn did a little casting around on his own.

He asked, "Have you got a key to your uncle's apartment in town?"

"Yes, I've had one for years. And one to his cottage, too. In case anything came up when he was away."

"Well, then, you could start by going to his apartment and looking for something that would tell you where he went. There's also the garage where he keeps his car. Maybe he spoke to the people there about where he was going. He did take his car, didn't he?"

"Why—" Glenn looked blank. "I don't know. He said he was going to drive to Vancouver—"

"But he didn't go to Vancouver. So the car is another thing you should check on right away."

Glenn nodded. "I'll go back to Hampton as soon as I've eaten." He eyed Jim questioningly. "I wonder if you'd mind—I don't like to ask you to give up your evening but—"

"You want me to go with you? All right. You go home and have your dinner and I'll have mine and then we'll leave."

This was the signal for the group to disperse. Margaret went inside to hurry dinner along and the others went to their respective cottages. Sarah and Loria rushed up to claim Jim's attention.

They led him to the washtub in a shady corner of the yard, wanting to share with him their grief over Bozo, a frog, missing from their aquatic collection.

"You sure he's gone?" Jim knelt to peer into the murky depths of the tub. "You sure he's not hidden under something?"

They shook their heads sorrowfully. "He's gone," Sarah said. "He hopped out, I guess. He was so cute, Daddy. When I called him by his name he recognized it."

"How could he hop out with this screen over the tub?" her father inquired.

"He did. He was getting so big and strong. He was the one I caught last spring, remember? He grew and grew and he was so strong I guess he pushed up the screen with his front legs and hopped out with his back legs."

Jim chose not to question the intricacies of this performance. He got to his feet, saying, "Well, it's too bad. You'd better weigh the screen down with some stones so it can't happen again."

"I'll get some right away." Sarah went off in search of them.

Juney emerged from the wood with unhurried tread and rubbed himself against Jim's leg. There were no bits of frog clinging to his whiskers, he purred and rubbed with an expression of innocent delight. Nevertheless, Jim regarded him with suspicion.

Loria, who had Margaret's dark blue eyes, looked up at her father wistfully. "Sarah said Bozo belonged just to her because she caught him. But he was my favorite frog too."

Jim squeezed her arm in sympathy. "It's a shame," he declared. "Maybe you can catch another one yourself."

"Oh, Daddy, will you help me?"

"I'll see."

"When? Now?"

"No, not now. But the first chance I get."

Jim helped the children set stones on the screen and

went back to the cottage with Sarah holding one of his hands and Loria the other. Margaret was putting dinner on the table.

The county detective had little to say during the meal. He was thinking about Leonard Riggott and the telephone call the latter had made to him. It had had no significance at the time; any trifling matter could have been the reason for it. But now he was connecting it with the date of the vandalism at his cottage. The call had been made the same day. When Riggott had asked him if he'd be in his office the next day he'd said yes. Instead, because of the vandalism, he'd gone to the lake. There'd been no further word from Riggott.

Jim's thoughts moved on to the steps to be taken next if tonight's trip to Hampton was fruitless. Riggott's finances would have to be investigated. He'd call Hildreth in the morning and ask him to inquire into them. A large withdrawal from Riggott's account around the time he went away would have meaning; or checks he'd cashed since might have been cleared through the bank; or, if he used traveler's checks, the bank might have a record of their serial numbers.

The possibility that Riggott was in financial hot water of some kind was uppermost in Jim's thoughts; he wouldn't be the first reputedly wealthy man to drop out of sight for that reason.

During the drive to Hampton the county detective let Glenn do the speculating about Leonard Riggott. He wasn't, he said, prepared to offer any theories as to what had become of him until he had more to go on.

"But the way he's disappeared," Glenn said. "It's quite unusual, isn't it?"

Jim was driving his car. He took his eyes off the road

to glance at the younger man whose narrow, beak-nosed face wore its most serious expression.

"I'm not even calling it a disappearance yet," he replied. "All we know is that your uncle didn't go to Vancouver as he had planned, that he hasn't been home, and you haven't heard from him in a couple of months. Let's not borrow trouble ahead of time."

"Well, if you put it that way—" Glenn subsided.

At the apartment they began their search in the bedroom. Glenn, looking in the closets, couldn't be sure what clothes his uncle had taken with him. "He had a raft of them," he explained. "It's hard to tell."

Leonard couldn't have taken many, Jim reflected. The closets were well filled.

A toothbrush hung in the rack in the bathroom, there were two razors, a shaving brush, and a tube of shaving cream in the medicine chest. It was quite likely that Riggott had a fitted kit for traveling, but still—

In the storage closet off the bedroom there were several pieces of luggage.

Glenn said, "I don't know how many he had."

"Trunks?"

"They'd be in the basement."

When they moved on to the den Glenn said he didn't know the combination of the safe. It was locked, Jim found, trying the door.

Presently he turned from the desk that had yielded no clues to Leonard's whereabouts and assessed the neatness of the room.

"Who does the cleaning here?" he asked.

"Uncle Len had maid service. It goes with the place if you want it."

"Well, we'll talk to the superintendent about it."

They found nothing anywhere in the apartment to interest them. When they were ready to leave Jim said, "What about your uncle's mail?"

"He didn't have it delivered here. He had a box at the post office."

"That can be checked tomorrow for a forwarding address." Jim paused in the foyer and looked around him. What else would give them a lead?

"Newspapers," he said. "We ought to be able to find out when he stopped delivery of them."

"I don't think he had a paper boy. He usually had breakfast in the coffee shop downstairs and he'd pick up his paper there."

"Uh-huh. I don't suppose he had milk delivered either. His kind of life has its drawbacks when it comes to trying to get a line on him. Let's go down and see what the superintendent can tell us."

The superintendent, a man in his forties, slow moving, slow talking and, Jim soon learned, slow thinking, had no information for them. He stood in his doorway—he didn't invite them inside—scratching his chest where a mat of gray hair showed through a thin jersey and made an effort to remember when he had last seen Leonard.

"Getting on toward the end of April it was," he said finally. "I knew he was going away. He'd spoke of it to me, but he didn't say just when."

"Did he make it a practice to go away without notifying you of the date of his departure or asking you to keep an eye on his place?" Jim inquired.

The man shrugged. "He didn't need to tell me nothing. He knew I'd look after things. He's been living here seven or eight years now and he's away a lot. Free as a bird, he is." There was a note of envy in the superintendent's voice as he said this that was, in view of the clamor of children's voices quarreling in the background, understandable.

"It wasn't like I had to turn the heat off or collect the rent or something," he added, after an interval devoted to scratching himself. "Everybody's got a lease in this building, they pay their rent only once or twice a year. Mr. Riggott, he pays his in February."

"I hear you furnish him with maid service."

"My wife takes care of Mr. Riggott's apartment."

"May I speak to her?" Jim asked. "Perhaps she can tell me something about him."

"I don't think so but—" Again the man shrugged. "No reason you can't speak to her if you want to." He turned and shouted, "C'mere, Carrie."

His wife appeared so promptly it was obvious she had been within eavesdropping distance.

"It's about Mr. Riggott," her husband informed her. "These gen'lmen, Mr. Riggott's nephew and a friend, are trying to find out where he went."

The woman turned a gaze no more alert than her husband's on Jim. "I don't know," she said.

"But you did know he was going away?"

"Oh yes, he spoke to me about it same as always. We have an understanding that when he's not there I'm to do his apartment just once a week."

"Then he'd tell you when he was leaving?"

"Well, usually he would. This time he didn't. I went up there one day a couple of months ago—a Sunday it was—and found the place the way I left it the day before. So I figured he'd gone off on his trip. I went back the next couple of days to make sure he was gone

80

and then I went on my once-a-week schedule."

The children's quarrel was getting louder. Jim had to raise his voice to make himself heard as he asked, "Does he just call you when he's back?"

"That's right. Joseph! Dicky! Eileen! Be quiet." The woman smiled apologetically at Jim. "Kids," she said.

He smiled back. "I know, I have two of my own." He was thinking, "If Sarah and Loria ever carried on like this bunch, I'd blister their bottoms for them."

He continued, "It seems rather casual that Mr. Riggott went away without notifying you."

"He's done it before. Not when he was gone as long as this, though," she added after a moment of rumination. "Other times when he didn't know he'd be gone maybe a week."

The county detective asked about pieces of luggage. Although the woman had been cleaning Leonard's apartment for years she didn't know how many pieces he had. "A lot," she declared with an air of helpfulness. "Six or seven or eight maybe. And two trunks. But they're in the basement storeroom. He didn't take them."

Questions about what clothes he might have taken elicited the same vagueness. She didn't know. "He has closets full of them," she said. "More than my husband ever seen in his life."

There was nothing more to be learned from the pair. Jim and Glenn went on to the garage. The Jaguar was there, they were told, Leonard hadn't taken it with him.

The garage attendant couldn't remember just when the car had last been used. It must be a couple of months, he said. No, they didn't keep track of dates with people who rented garage space on an annual basis. Mr. Riggott's car was there, they serviced it, but there was no reason he should keep them informed of his plans. No, the attendant said, he couldn't begin to remember when he had last seen Mr. Riggott.

After they left the garage Jim said, "What about his club? He was there quite often, wasn't he?"

"Oh yes, he had lunch or dinner or played bridge there three or four times a week."

"He'd sign the checks for his meals," Jim said.

They drove to the Hampton Club. The manager looked up Leonard Riggott's account. The last meal charged to him was dinner on April 23.

There was no more they could do that night. They started back to the lake.

"We didn't find out a thing," Glenn observed. "Not one blessed thing."

Jim didn't agree with him. He thought the negative aspects of the evening had served to highlight the completeness of Leonard's disappearance—he was calling it that to himself now—and that unless they got a forwarding address from the post office tomorrow or information from Leonard's bank that would tell them where he was, he would have to be declared missing.

The county detective kept these thoughts to himself. He told Glenn that in the morning he would call Lieutenant Hildreth of the Hampton Detective Bureau and ask him to make a few inquiries.

"Like at the post office, you mean?"

"Yes. And his bank. Where does he have his account?"

"The Hampton Trust Company."

"We'll see what they can tell us," Jim said.

He didn't yet have a sense of urgency about Leonard.

He was waiting on the next day's developments.

When he reached his office in the morning he called Lieutenant Hildreth. The latter wasn't enthusiasic over his request. He was pretty busy, he said, and while Jim didn't want this guy reported missing officially, he wanted the same kind of work done to locate him. Having made his complaints, he added, "But I'll see what I can do. As a favor to you. Strictly on that basis and expecting the favor returned when I need it."

"I knew you'd say that," Jim told him. "It just goes to show. I never got something for nothing in my life and I never will."

"Of course not," the lieutenant replied. "Why should you? I'll give you a ring as soon as I have anything on it."

"Okay." Jim hung up and looked at his watch. He was due to testify this morning in the case of the State versus Anthony Carmichael, the last case on the docket before the summer adjournment. Court would be opening soon. He'd better get downstairs.

Seven

Late that afternoon Lieutenant Hildreth, instead of phoning the county detective, came to see him at his office. As soon as he was seated he said, "I don't think you'll find Riggott with any unofficial pussyfooting around. I haven't been able to uncover one trace of him after the April 24 date you gave me."

He went on to tell Jim what he had done. Calls to the airport, railroad station, cab companies, bus stations had brought no results. The post office had no forwarding address for Leonard Riggott and a great stack of mail had been piling up for him, the earliest postmark on any of it being April 24.

From the post office, Hildreth said, he had gone to Leonard's bank. His ledger card showed no checks written against his account since April 22.

"He cashed a check for eleven hundred dollars that day," Hildreth continued. "Out of it he bought a thousand dollars' worth of traveler's checks, each one for fifty dollars. I got the serial numbers on them. Then I found out that the last ones he bought before that were last December. The bank said the checks came from the American Express Company and wherever they were cashed they'd eventually get back to the company's office in New York. So I called the New York office—and somebody's going to have to pay for that call and also for the collect call they made back to me just before I came over here. I can't charge off unofficial inquiries to the department. How about it?" He looked at Jim with a firm eye.

"All right," Jim said. "You present the bill and I'll hang it on Saxton. What'd you find out from them?"

"That not one of the checks Riggott bought in April has been cleared through their office. He'd cashed all but two of the ones he bought in December. He'd used them up, all but the two, on some trip he took then. They're still to be accounted for besides the ones he bought in April. We don't know, of course, how much cash he had on him along with the hundred he drew that day at the bank. But it couldn't have been too much. His card showed no large withdrawals for months back, only about what you'd expect them to be with a guy that had his kind of dough. So," the lieutenant concluded, "that brings up the question of what he's been eating on the last couple of months."

"It sure does," Jim said.

"Unless he's got another account somewhere else."

"Why should he have?"

"Well, if he was mixed up in something shady, he could have another account maybe under a different name."

"I doubt there was anything like that. Tad Beecher, another neighbor of mine at the lake, is his broker and he's said things from time to time that indicate Riggott has plenty of money. What was his balance at the bank?"

"It ran over five thousand."

"Well, he lives on invested money and he's pretty shrewd and careful. From what I know of him I'd say he's the perennial bachelor, very fond of himself, likes to think he's something of a playboy, but is actually a pretty conservative, cautious kind of fellow. He wouldn't have any reason to get mixed up in anything shady and I don't think he's the type to do it."

"You said he was a playboy. You mean women—or did he play around with other boys?" The lieutenant grinned at Jim.

"I meant women. I'd say he was a perfectly normal man."

"Maybe he was mixed up with some woman then and she was making things hot for him."

"Yes." Jim thought of Loretta Madler but didn't mention her. "But regardless of why he dropped out of sight, what's he using for money?"

That, they decided, was, for the moment, the heart of the matter. When they had talked it over Jim said, "He called me April 23," and went on to tell the lieutenant about Leonard's call and the vandalism at his cottage that night, which had fixed the date in his mind.

"You think there's a connection between the call and his disappearance?"

"There could be." Jim spoke slowly. "And what about the vandalism?"

"I don't see how that ties in. The call to you could mean he was in trouble even if he didn't seem to be in too big a hurry to see you about it. But the vandalism is something else."

86

"Just a thought I had," Jim said.

Presently the lieutenant stood up to leave. "I think it's time to quit horsing around on this," he stated. "His nephew ought not to lose any more time in reporting him missing."

"I'm going to tell him to do it right away."

"Then I'll expect to hear from him on it." Hildreth picked up his hat and set it on the back of his head. "So long."

"So long. And thanks a lot."

"You're welcome. Just do the same for me one of these days." The lieutenant made his departure.

At first, when the county detective called Glenn at his office, the latter hesitated over reporting his uncle missing. "It'll get in the papers," he objected. "With a man like Uncle Len they'll give it a big play and then, if he is all right, he'll be furious at me. Honestly, Jim, I don't like to take the responsibility for it. Can't I let it go a little longer?"

"No, you can't," Jim said flatly. "It's gone too long already. If you're worried about what your uncle will say, I'm prepared to tell him I insisted you do it."

"All right," said Glenn. "I'll go to police headquarters and see Lieutenant Hildreth."

That night Leonard Riggott's disappearance was on the six-thirty news broadcast. Jim and Margaret heard it at their dinner table; the Beechers and Lipscombs next door heard it; Loretta Madler, eating from a tray with a book open beside her, heard it; Nicky Saxton, waiting for Glenn to get home, heard it; Glenn himself, on his way to the lake, heard it on his car radio.

It had a subduing effect on all of them to listen to the announcer saying, ". . . member of a well-known

Hampton family . . . Community Chest Board . . . trustee of Hampton General Hospital . . . director of Hampton Electronics Company . . . Curtis Lockridge Corporation . . . Height, five feet eight, weight, approximately one hundred and fifty pounds, blue eyes . . . Anyone having any knowledge of Mr. Riggott's whereabouts is urged to get in touch with the Hampton Police Department immediately . . ."

At eight o'clock that evening Tad, Dean, and Glenn gathered with Jim on his dock to ask him questions about how missing-persons cases were handled.

Dean made it a point to ask as many questions as the others. It was easy enough for him to adopt a sober expression. His long period of grace, much longer than he had expected, was drawing to an end; the hunt was on for the man he had murdered.

As they talked he even found himself wishing he could hasten the discovery of the body by calling attention to Leonard's cottage. The sooner the murder investigation began the sooner it would end.

He listened to the way Jim answered each question, his voice quiet, patient, weighing his answers. In the few weeks Dean had known the county detective he had come to realize the latter had much intelligence, persistence, ability. But still Dean felt confident he was safe enough, that Jim would find no reason to turn his attention to him. He felt confident but nervous, like a man facing a serious operation, knowing it will be successful and yet wanting to get it over with.

When the hue and cry died down Dean meant to leave Hampton. He would tell Tad Elaine wasn't happy there and that they were going back to Philadelphia. Tad would question the wisdom of Dean's giving in to

Elaine's wishes, but he wouldn't look for another reason for Dean's departure.

Dean had fixed on September as the month when he could go without arousing suspicion. In Philadelphia he would look around for some promising small business in which he could buy a partnership. Elaine and he, their days of financial stress behind them, would settle down and at last be happy together. He would, in time, be able to forget Leonard Riggott.

A vagrant thought, that Elaine would never be happy anywhere with him, struck Dean just then. He thrust it from his mind, but it left him with the feeling that he must see her immediately, assure himself that she was still within reach on the Beecher porch where she had been when he walked down to the dock with Tad.

He waited for a lull in the conversation and said, "Well, I guess I'll go see what Elaine is doing."

That's what they would expect to hear from him, he knew. His devotion to his wife was no secret from anyone. Doglike devotion, he corrected himself with a tinge of bitterness as he headed back to the Beecher cottage.

Elaine was on the porch turning over the pages of a magazine.

"Where's Mrs. Beecher?" Dean asked.

"Oh, she went over to see Margaret again." Elaine dropped the magazine and glanced up at her husband, her lovely face quite without expression. "Let's get out of here for a while," she said. "I'm tired of looking at the lake."

"D'you think it's all right? Considering—?"

Her eyes widened. "Heaven's sake, why not? You

hardly knew Mr. Riggott and I never laid eyes on him myself. His disappearance has nothing to do with us."

"All right." He spoke quickly. "Let's go."

The three men on the dock watched them drive away in their car. Tad shook his head. "She's sure got him wrapped around her finger. Wants to be on the go every night in the week and he doesn't dare refuse."

Glenn looked at his watch. It was eight-thirty; the sun was low in the west. "If they're going to that drive-in on the valley road, they'll just about be in time for the show." He added, "You'd think she'd let him stay home tonight. In case anything comes up."

"Not her," Tad declared. "She comes first with herself every day in the week and twice on Sunday."

They were sitting on Jim's dock. Tonight no one suggested going fishing or for a ride around the lake in Tad's motorboat.

Silence settled on them. They could hear the women talking on the O'Neill porch, and the shrill voices of Tommy Saxton and Loria playing on the steps. They could see Sarah in the swing in the back yard with Juney on her lap and Rex at her feet.

"It's time those kids were in bed," Jim remarked.

"Yeah," Glenn agreed. "Things seem kind of upset tonight, though."

There was another silence. Jim found that his gaze kept fastening on the closed-up cottage next door. Len, he reflected, hadn't been near the place since last fall— so far as he knew. Glenn had gone through it that day in April when they were all at the lake. Glenn had a key to it.

The county detective turned this fact over in his mind. It was pleasant sitting there on the dock while a tranquil June day came to an end. He had no inclination to bestir himself for a search of Leonard's cottage.

He watched a sailboat skim past with the last rays of the sun reddening its sails. It was a pretty thing to see. He turned his head to keep it in view.

They'd gone to Riggott's apartment last night, they really ought to take a look around his cottage, Jim thought. They wouldn't be apt to find anything there, but still—

"Glenn," he said, "you got the key to your uncle's cottage handy?"

"Yes, it's at my place."

"Will you get it, please? I think we ought to take a look around over there."

"Whatever you say." The younger man stood up and went after the key.

Tad said, "I don't think Len's been near the place since last fall."

"Neither do I," the county detective replied. "However—"

Glenn returned with the key and they walked over to the cottage.

Jim took the key and opened the back door. As they stepped over the threshold the smell of putrefaction assailed them. . . .

Eight

Jim sent the others back outside. He had to get a flashlight to find his way through the shuttered cottage and upstairs to Leonard's room. He stood in the doorway, his handkerchief held to his nose, while he played the light over the grisly thing on the floor and then sent its beam around the disordered room. He did not linger. He went downstairs and out the way he had come, closing and locking the back door after him.

Tad and Glenn were standing at the foot of the steps. They looked up at him in white-faced silence.

Jim gulped fresh air and said, "He's been there a long time."

"God, how awful." Glenn gave a convulsive shudder. "And all the while we've been right here going about our affairs, Uncle Len—" He broke off looking as if he might be sick at any moment.

"Did you—have you any idea what happened to him?" Tad asked.

"I didn't stick around long enough to find out," Jim said briefly. "Well—" He gave himself a little shake and came down the steps glancing out over the lake where lights had begun to dot the opposite shore. The scene was peaceful, the water purple in the twilight, a shred of new moon low in the sky. Light streamed from the window of his cottage next door, the laughter of a girl in a boat came clear and gay across the water.

In a short time Jim knew all of it would change. Police cars would arrive, a great bustle of activity would be centered around what was left of Leonard Riggott.

Tad and Glenn hurried off to tell their wives Leonard was dead, Jim went back to his cottage to use the telephone. He was glad to find the other women gone and Margaret alone in the living room after having put the children to bed.

She said, "Oh no," when he told her about Leonard, but she didn't start flinging questions at him. She sat quietly while he phoned the state police barracks, Goodrich, the state's attorney, the nearest medical examiner, and then, as a matter of courtesy, the Garfield constable, High Point Lake being part of the village.

When he turned away from the telephone Margaret said in a hushed voice, "Jim, the children have been over there any number of times; I've had to call them back when they were playing on the porch. And all the while he was inside there. If they'd been able to get in, they would have found him."

"Don't think about that." He stood up. "I'll go back over and wait for the reinforcements to arrive."

She detained him a moment longer. "From what you said on the phone—he was murdered, wasn't he?"

"It looks like it." Jim didn't caution her, "Don't

mention it to the others." He knew she wouldn't.

He went back to the other cottage and sat on the steps waiting for the state police who were near at hand and would get there long before anyone from the state's attorney's office.

It was dark by this time. He was not given to flights of imagination, but Leonard's body had had its effect on him. He found himself peopling the deeper darkness of the wood on the far side of the cottage with moving figures, although common sense told him none was there; only the fireflies drifting in and out among the trees. Once he even got to his feet and walked to the edge of the wood to take a closer look at a peculiarly shaped black shadow. It was a tall straggly bush, he discovered, and went back to the steps feeling a trifle foolish.

Nevertheless, he was pleased when he saw Tad and Glenn coming toward him.

They reported that the women were in tears and very much upset. Loretta, they said, was crying hardest of all.

"What about lights in this place?" Jim inquired of Glenn.

"The current is on all year. Uncle Len just threw off the main switch in the garage when he closed up in the fall."

"Will the police be here soon?" asked Tad.

"Any minute." As Jim spoke he caught a glimpse of lights on the lake road. "Here they are now, I think." He got to his feet taking the key to the cottage out of his pocket.

There were two cars arriving. When they stopped in the driveway Tad said, "Well, I guess you won't want us underfoot for a while," and Glenn and he retreated from the scene.

Lieutenant Schmidt headed the state police contingent. With him were a photographer, a fingerprint man, and two troopers.

While they were getting out of their cars a third car came into view. In this one was the Garfield constable.

Jim unlocked the back door and led the way into the cottage.

"My God," the lieutenant exclaimed, as soon as he was inside. "Kelly"—he turned to one of his subordinates—"open all the doors and windows."

They got the lights turned on before they went upstairs, Jim again leading the way. This time he went into the room and opened the windows. Someone else opened the rest of the upstairs windows.

The photographer and fingerprint man went valiantly to work. Schmidt and Jim and the constable, after looking at the body and making a quick inspection of the other rooms, went downstairs.

The next car to arrive held the medical examiner, a youngish brisk man who lost some of his briskness once he was inside. But he didn't skimp on his job. He spent considerable time in his examination of the body. When he came downstairs his first action was to wash his hands thoroughly—one of the troopers had located the main valve of the water supply and turned it on—and then he was ready to talk to Jim and the lieutenant and the constable.

They went out on the front porch and grouped themselves along the railing.

The medical examiner said, "I can't tell you too much. You'll have to wait for the autopsy report for most of what you'll want to know. The condition of the body . . ." His voice trailed off, picked up vitality again. "There's a wound in the chest that looks like a knife or bullet wound. That's the only one I found. The man's been dead, I'd say, between two and three months. That's about as close as anyone will be able to come to it."

"He was last known to be alive on April 24, Doctor," Jim informed him. "Would you say he must have died very close to that date?"

The medical examiner nodded. "I'd say very close indeed, that he couldn't have been alive much longer—assuming, of course, that he was placed in the room upstairs soon after death and that the cottage has been kept closed up ever since."

Jim and the lieutenant looked at him. It was the lieutenant who said, "Placed there? The body was moved after death?"

"Oh yes. I can be definite about that. Discoloration is all on the right side of the body. If death had occurred while it was in its present position, the discoloration would be on the left side. I never try to pin post-mortem lividity down too close, but for some period, at least four or five hours after death, the position of the body was the reverse of what it is now."

The medical examiner's tone was casual in putting the stamp of murder on Leonard's death. He had nothing more to tell them. He said, "About the autopsy—Eisenberg at Hampton General?"

"Fine," Jim agreed.

"I'll have to call the coroner first."

"I have a phone at my place next door." Jim took him to his cottage to call the coroner and then the pathologist at the hospital in Hampton. After that, with Jim consulting Glenn's preference, a Hampton undertaker was called to remove the body.

The lake road was lined with cars when the medical examiner and Jim came out of the O'Neill cottage. A state trooper was stationed at the end of the road keeping the onlookers at a distance.

Detectives Cobb and Bailo had arrived and were talking with Lieutenant Schmidt and the constable.

"Some deal," Cobb greeted Jim, when the latter had seen the medical examiner to his car and joined the group.

"I like my murders brand new," Cobb continued. He was a big, phlegmatic-looking man, unhurried in speech and movement. Beside him Bailo, years younger, with a dark mobile face, appeared even shorter and slighter than he was.

"You been upstairs?" Jim inquired.

"I went, but I didn't see no call to hang around up there. How soon are they going to take it away?"

"The hearse should be on its way now."

"Eisenberg going to do the autopsy?" asked Bailo.

"Yes."

"Hell of a way he's got for earning his living."

"Ours doesn't always strike me as so good either," Jim commented.

"It looks like a tough case," Schmidt said and added aggrievedly, "How can you really go into action when you don't even know when a murder took place?"

"At least we know approximately when," the county detective said. "Around April 24. Around the time my cottage was vandalized." After a pause he went on, "You never did find the teen-agers who were supposed

97

to have done it. In fact all you ever had that pointed to them was the story of some anonymous motorist."

"I know," Schmidt said, going along with Jim's train of thought. "I questioned every kid for miles around that's ever been in any kind of trouble, but it got me nowhere."

"Maybe we'd better take a fresh look at it when we get a chance," Jim observed. "In the meantime, let's get organized." His glance went to Cobb and Bailo. "We'll start with Riggott's movements on Saturday, April 24. You two take the Hampton end, the other tenants in the apartment house, the members and staff of the Hampton Club, the attendants at the garage where Riggott kept his car, and so on. Try to pin down the superintendent's wife on when she went up to clean Riggott's apartment and found it unused. She thinks it was a Sunday."

Cobb shook his head. "Most people when you question them about dates, they can't hardly remember what happened yesterday. But you want them to remember what happened two months ago. Miracles is what you're looking for, Jim."

The latter grinned at the big detective. "All right, miracles then."

"You're going to take on the nephew and the other people out here?" Bailo inquired.

"The lieutenant and I will start on them as soon as we get the body off our hands." Jim's glance went to the village constable who knew he was out of his depth and, like the sensible man he was, had been keeping quiet.

Three of them appearing together to ask questions would be too many, Jim reflected. On the other hand, the murder had been committed—or at least the body had been found—within the constable's domain, and much stress was laid on cooperation between the law-enforcement agencies. The county detective felt he had no choice but to say, "Would you care to come along, Constable, when we talk to these people?"

The constable gave a further demonstration of his good sense by replying, "No thanks. I think three of us would be quite a crowd." He smiled self-deprecatingly at Jim. "To tell you the truth, Mr. O'Neill, this whole thing is a little rich for my blood. I've never come up against a murder case before, not in all the years I've been constable. But if there's anything I can do to help I'd be only too glad to do it."

"There is a job you can do better than any of us," Jim told him. "Make inquiries around the village. Riggott was well known there. You might find out something that would be helpful."

The constable nodded, pleased to have been assigned a task within the scope of his abilities. "I'll see what I can do," he said, "and let you know what I find out."

"Fine. Keep in touch with me."

"I will. And as long as you don't need me here I'll get back to the village now." The constable said good night and left.

Cobb and Bailo left for Hampton a few minutes later. In another few minutes the hearse arrived and Leonard Riggott's body was started on its way to the pathologist at Hampton General.

The state police technicians had completely taken over the cottage. Jim and the lieutenant were free to begin the question-and-answer routine that would go on until the murder was solved.

They went first to Glenn Saxton's where they found Glenn and his wife, the Beechers, and Loretta Madler sitting in a solemn circle talking in the low voices that death, violent or natural, seems to demand.

Jim was glad to see that Margaret, knowing he would appear here in his official capacity, was not part of the group.

He introduced Schmidt. While Glenn stood aside Tad took over the duties of a host, pulling chairs forward and telling them to sit down and make themselves comfortable. His instinct for good fellowship, which could never be long repressed, lent social aspects to their arrival.

It wouldn't do, Jim reflected; there were drawbacks as well as advantages to being on friendly terms with people you had to question in a murder investigation.

"Have you found out yet what caused Len's death?" asked Tad.

Jim shook his head. "His body has been taken away for autopsy, but we won't know how he died until we have the pathologist's report. All the medical examiner would say was that he'd been dead two or three months."

The word murder wasn't going to come into the conversation tonight, Jim and the lieutenant had decided ahead of time. It would tighten these people up when what they wanted was to have them talk freely.

"We know he didn't die three months ago," the county detective continued. "He was alive as recently as the twenty-fourth of April. What we want to do first is to try to establish the actual date of his death and whatever else we can connected with it."

He paused while his glance went over them. "I don't

100

suppose there's anyone who was closer to Len than the five of you."

Loretta said, "I wasn't close to him. Not at the time of his death."

"You were before that, though," Jim pointed out. He went on, "I want all of you to think hard about the last time you saw him, how he acted, what he said and did, particularly anything that, when you look back on it, would indicate he was bothered by some problem. I think he was. He called me on Friday, April 23, to ask me if he could see me at my office the next day. That was my last contact with him."

Jim was alert for a reaction to what he was saying. Lieutenant Schmidt was looking for one too. But all they saw on the five faces was surprise.

"You've never mentioned his call before," Tad said.

"No, I treated it as confidential."

"Why didn't he go to your office the next day?" Nicky inquired.

"I wasn't there. I was up here cleaning up my cottage after the vandalism of the night before."

Oh, it was that time . . . Did he call your office?"

"No, he knew from Lieutenant Schmidt that I'd be up here."

"But if he wanted to see you about something important he could have called you the following Monday," Glenn suggested.

"If he was still alive then. We don't know that he was. Your conversation with him on the phone that Saturday morning was the last direct knowledge we have of him alive."

Everyone's eyes went to Glenn. He made a gesture that repudiated their glances. "All we talked about was

101

my looking over his cottage. Lieutenant Schmidt had just called him."

"I remember you went through his cottage that day," Tad said.

"Yes. It was all right then."

There was no reason why it shouldn't have been, Jim thought. Riggott hadn't been murdered yet.

He had been murdered, though, very soon thereafter. In all probability, that same day or night.

He said, "I think we'll make headway faster if the lieutenant and I talk to you separately. It will give all of us a chance to concentrate."

"Whatever you say, Jim," Tad replied.

"Well, then, you and Phoebe wait for us at your place and Loretta at hers and we can begin here with Glenn and Nicky."

"All right," Tad said. He left with the two women. Jim, who had been standing all this time, sat down beside Schmidt and took out his notebook. His investigation was under way.

Nine

He began by asking general questions about the dead man's friends and the customary pattern of his activities.

Nicky supplied most of the answers. Glenn had little to say until he asked a question of his own: "Do you suppose Uncle Len had a heart attack?"

"Had he ever complained of his heart?"

"No, but sometimes people have them without warning. That's what we were talking about before you came in; that he was alone in his cottage and had one."

"How do you figure he got there without his car?"

"Perhaps someone drove him out and left before he had the attack."

"How was he supposed to get home from there?"

"I don't know." Glenn looked taken aback. "I hadn't thought about that."

"Well, it's something that requires thought." Jim dismissed speculation about the cause of Leonard's death by asking, "What happened between your uncle and Loretta Madler?"

"I guess he just got tired of her. Sooner or later he always got tired of the women he went around with." Glenn didn't enlarge on the statement in an effort to direct suspicion at Loretta.

But then, the county detective reminded himself, Glenn didn't know as yet that it was a murder case. Not unless he had committed the murder himself.

He went on to questions about the dead man's financial affairs. The latter had inherited all his parents' money, Glenn said. His mother, Leonard's sister, had died when Glenn was a baby and his father, having quarreled with Glenn's grandparents, had left Hampton. When his father died twelve years ago, Glenn continued, he had got in touch with his uncle. After the war the latter got him a job in the advertising department of the Hampton Electronics Company. Three years ago, with Hampton Electronics as his first and biggest account, Glenn had opened the Saxton Advertising Agency. His uncle had advanced him a few thousand for the venture and his agency was now grossing thirty thousand a year.

To Jim, asking questions about gross and net and doing figures in his head, this sounded substantial enough. But also in his head was a hazy memory of something Margaret had mentioned about Nicky's worry that Glenn might lose his biggest account.

"Who inherits your uncle's estate?" he inquired.

Glenn flushed a little. "According to what Uncle Len told me, half of it comes to me and the other half goes to Hampton General Hospital. My grandfather was one of its founders and the bequest is to set up a memorial in his memory."

"Who is executor of his will?"

"The Hampton Trust Company."

The Saxtons were sitting side by side on a sofa, Glenn with an embarrassed expression, Nicky trying to look as if her thoughts were above such things as the money they would inherit from Leonard Riggott.

"No financial reverses so far as you know?" Jim asked.

"Oh no."

"Did he ever say anything that would indicate he was in any other kind of trouble? Someone with resentful feelings or some kind of hold on him?"

"Nothing like that," Glenn and Nicky replied in unison. Then, his sandy eyebrows knitted in thought, Glenn added, "You make it sound as if someone had—well, a grudge against him."

Jim saw Schmidt stare at the younger man, his eyebrows edging up in disbelief that so much naïveté could be genuine.

"We don't know about that yet," was the reply the county detective made. He stood up to leave. He felt there was little to be gained by prolonging the interview tonight; it was getting late and he had to see the others.

He said, "We can go into more detail about this tomorrow. You'll be around, won't you, Glenn?"

"I suppose I'll be back and forth. I'll have to go in to Hampton to see the undertaker about funeral arrangements. There'll be any number of things to take care of and they'll all be up to me." Glenn looked harassed as he spoke.

"Well, don't think about them until tomorrow. Good night . . . Good night, Nicky."

"Good night." There was constraint in Nicky's tone. It had come suddenly, bred of her thoughts.

They'd all be constrained with him from now on, Jim reflected as Schmidt and he left. They'd be seeing him in a different light.

When they were away from the cottage the lieutenand said meditatively, "The guy that inherits the dough. Number one motive for murder."

"Number two motive, the woman that got ditched," Jim answered, turning toward Loretta's.

Her manner was detached at the beginning of their talk with her. She said Leonard and she had seen a lot of each other for a while, they had had good times together, she had enjoyed his company.

Jim said, "Around here, we thought you were both getting pretty serious about each other."

Her voice sharpened as she replied, "I can't imagine why. Certainly we were mature enough to have a friendship without being starry-eyed over it. I'm sure I had no thought of marrying Len. From the start of our acquaintance I knew he was a confirmed bachelor."

She looked straight at Jim while she said this. But her voice shook slightly, her whole look was ravaged. She lived on her emotions, he recognized. Reason, with her, would be subjugated to them; the maturity she spoke of went only skin-deep.

She elaborated on the platonic character of her relationship with Leonard, talking quickly, making too many gestures. Schmidt regarded her imperturbably.

When she came to a halt Jim asked, "When did you last see him?"

"Well . . ." Loretta hesitated, remembering vividly the last time she had seen the dead man. She had phoned him, desperate with the knowledge he was finished with her. She had talked hysterically, threaten-

106

ing to go up to his apartment and make a scene. Her tactics had been the very worst she could have used with a man like Len. He had come down to her apartment to quiet her, but he had stayed only ten or fifteen minutes, telling her Dean Lipscomb was upstairs and he had to get back to him. . . .

Perhaps he had told Dean who was calling; perhaps he had even said something dreadful about her making a nuisance of herself. He was quite capable of it. She had known for a long time that he could be very cruel and self-centered, but she'd shut her eyes to this side of his nature and gone on hoping against hope—

When he came to her apartment that night he said he'd take her to lunch the next day and they could then have a talk. He hadn't shown up. He'd sent some flowers and on the card enclosed with them had been a message, "Sorry, can't make it today. Will call you."

She had gone to pieces over it. Right in front of Ann Streicher who had dropped in on her just before the flowers were delivered.

Len hadn't called her. She'd tried to call him several times that week and the next, but either there'd been no answer or the creature who cleaned his apartment had come on the phone and said he wasn't there. The following week when he must have already been dead, she had again tried to reach him. Gradually she'd given up . . .

She said, "The last time I saw him was around the middle of April and then it was only for a few minutes. He ran down to my apartment—he couldn't stay, he said, because Dean Lipscomb was visiting him—and suggested we have lunch together. We were both quite busy, though, and we didn't get around to it. That was the last time I saw him."

Neither Jim not the lieutenant offered a comment. Loretta felt impelled to add, "We hadn't been seeing much of each other for quite a while before that. Not since late in the winter."

"What happened?" the county detective asked.

She shrugged and brought forth what was meant to be a light laugh. "Just one of those things. After all, I had other men friends and Len, I suppose, had other women friends."

She lit a cigarette, feeling pleased with the way she was handling the interview, removing from her account of her association with Leonard everything that would suggest she had been discarded by him.

The two men appeared to accept what she had told them at its face value. Jim asked her the same questions he had asked the Saxtons about Leonard's behavior, whether or not he had seemed worried about anything, or had spoken of anyone harboring ill feeling toward him.

Loretta said no. She studied Jim. "How did he die actually?"

"I don't know yet." Jim got to his feet. "Thanks very much. I'll see you later. You'll be right here at the lake, of course."

"Yes."

"Okay then. Good night."

"Good night." She stood in the doorway looking after them.

The Beechers were waiting in their living room. Tad asked if they'd like a drink. Lieutenant Schmidt said, "No thanks," and Jim softened his refusal by explaining that he never took a drink when he was working.

They didn't spend much time with the Beechers. The county detective already knew what they would say. He had heard it earlier that evening before Leonard's body was found. Tad had said Leonard made it a practice to stop in at Beecher's once or twice a week, but he couldn't remember exactly when he had last done it. Phoebe hadn't seen him since he had been to dinner at their house early in April.

Neither had noticed any signs of strain or anxiety in the man who was dead.

When they were outside headed for Jim's cottage the lieutenant said, "He could have been cutting himself in on Riggott's investments. And then, if Riggott found out and threatened him with exposure—"

"Yes, it's a point." Jim's tone was noncommittal. He liked Tad the best of all his lake neighbors.

Although it was nearly midnight Margaret was waiting up for her husband and had sandwiches and coffee ready. While they ate the two men talked about what they would do tomorrow. Lieutenant Schmidt would take the lake and the village, the county detective would work from the Hampton end. The lieutenant brought out Leonard's key case, which had been found in his room.

The telephone rang. Jim picked up the receiver. Cobb was calling him.

He said, "We've seen all the people we can tonight. We're signing off now."

"Any luck?"

"Nothing from the tenants we've talked to so far. But the superintendent's wife, she was some help. I kept after her about that Sunday she found Riggott's bed not slept in and finally she remembered it was the

Sunday Daylight Time came in. She forgot to turn her clock ahead, she said, and she was late all that morning with her work. That would make it Sunday, April 25."

"We never get away from that week end, do we?" Jim commented. "Who did you see at the garage?"

"The same guy you talked to last night, the one that don't hardly know enough to find his way back and forth to work. But there's two others that come on in the daytime and we'll talk to them tomorrow." Cobb paused before he added, "Not that it will do us any good."

"Probably not," Jim agreed. "Most things don't. But every now and then one of them does and that's what keeps us going. Thanks for calling. See you tomorrow."

He turned from the phone and told Schmidt what Cobb had learned from the superintendent's wife.

"It's beginning to look pretty conclusive that Riggott died April 24," Schmidt observed.

"And maybe fairly early in the day," Jim pointed out. "That is, if Saxton is telling the truth about having tried to call him when he got back from the lake that afternoon."

Schmidt nodded. "If he's telling the truth."

Dean arrived at Jim's cottage a few minutes later. Elaine was with him. They had gone to a drive-in movie, they said, and were so shocked to hear about Leonard when they got back to the lake.

Jim introduced the lieutenant and asked them to sit down. Margaret poured coffee for them.

"Mr. Beecher thought we'd better run over," Dean

said. "He told us you'd questioned all of them and might want to talk to us."

"Well, yes, to you," Jim replied. "But your wife wasn't living in Hampton at the time of Riggott's death." His glance moved on to Elaine. "Did you ever meet him?"

She shook her head. "He's just a name to me."

Margaret was studying Elaine thinking how attractive she looked tonight, her face alert and interested instead of showing its usual expression of boredom.

Jim had returned his attention to Dean. "I understand you spent an evening with Riggott not long before he disappeared. When was this?"

Dean adopted an earnest look. He meant to be perfectly honest about the night of his dinner engagement with Leonard right up to the point where he had stolen the bonds. Then, in case someone remembered seeing him go to Leonard's at a later date, he'd add something to cover it.

He began, "It was near the middle of April, I'd say," and went on to tell the county detective about having dinner at the Hampton Club, returning to Leonard's apartment, and being there when the call came from Loretta Madler. For Schmidt's benefit he digressed to explain the reasons for Leonard's display of friendly interest in him. The older man, he said, had taken him to lunch two or three times before he had asked him to have dinner with him. That night Leonard had seemed to be in good spirits except for being a little annoyed over the call from Mrs. Madler. "At least," Dean added with the air of wanting to be scrupulously exact, "I got the impression he was a little annoyed. More from his tone than from anything he said."

"What did he say?" Jim inquired.

"I can't begin to remember. But he sounded annoyed. Then, after he'd hung up, he told me she wanted to see him for a minute. He said he'd be right back and went down to her apartment. I looked at a magazine while he was gone. He was back inside of fifteen minutes. We had a drink and talked for about half an hour and then I went home."

"And except when Mrs. Madler called him, he was in good spirits the whole evening?"

"Yes, he was being very pleasant to me. That's why I feel so bad about his death," Dean explained with a solemn expression. "He went out of his way to be nice to me when I had no real claim on him."

Jim accepted this appropriate sentiment with a nod. Then he asked, "Was that the last time you saw him?"

"No, he invited me to drop in for a drink a few days later."

"About how many days later?"

Dean wrinkled his brow in a semblance of thought. "For the life of me I can't remember. A few days is as close as I can come."

Elaine supplied helpfully, "You didn't mention having a drink with him, but you did say he'd taken you out to dinner—shortly before you came to Philadelphia Easter week end. You must have had the drink with him after that. You remember, that was the week end you brought me my—" Elaine stopped just in time. She had started to say "my ring," momentarily forgetting that Dean had cautioned her against telling anyone it was new. He'd said Tad wouldn't like it that he'd been playing the market and had got the money to buy it that way. She finished lamely, "—the new charm for my bracelet."

Margaret looked at the gold bracelet with its four dangling charms: an exquisite little ballet dancer that commemorated the night Elaine had accepted Dean's proposal after attending the ballet with him; the wedding ring he had added to it when they were married; the airplane with revolving propeller blades that had been his farewell gift when he was sent to North Africa; and the new charm, the car he had bought out of Leonard's money.

Bracelets like that could run into fabulous sums, Margaret reflected, but Elaine was the type to like them and not concern herself with what they cost; and Dean was the type to go ahead and buy one for her. Which of the charms was new? Not the wedding ring, the least expensive of them, which must date back to their marriage. One of the others had been his Easter gift to his wife.

Elaine's diamond ring didn't draw Margaret's attention. She assumed it was an engagement ring. Elaine had been wearing it ever since they'd met.

Dean said quickly, "Oh yes, I remember. Well, if I didn't have a drink with Len that week it must have been right after I got back from Philadelphia."

"Which would be the week he disappeared," Jim remarked.

"Yes, I imagine so." Dean spoke in the same quick tone. He wanted to hurry through this fabrication of his and be done with it.

"Was it in the evening?" Jim asked.

"No, he called me and suggested I stop by after work for a drink. So I stopped and we had two drinks. I wasn't there long, though. I think he was going out."

113

"He didn't say where?"

Dean, who had been unnerved by Elaine's unexpected intervention, felt he was letting his story of the drink get away from him. He wished he hadn't used it at all. It was cover for his later visit that he probably hadn't needed and it violated his determination to tell as much of the truth as he could, eliminating where he must, but keeping the whole thing simple and straightforward. In that approach lay safety, he thought.

Still speaking quickly he said, "I don't know that he was going out. But he said he had to change so I left. That was the last time I saw him and he acted the same as before, not worried or anything."

"He didn't say whether his date was with a man or a woman?"

"He didn't say he had a date at all. He just said he had to change."

"What was he wearing?"

Dean found it an effort to keep edginess out of his voice as he replied, "A suit. I don't remember what color it was."

"I'm wondering if he meant he had to change into a dinner jacket," Jim explained. "That would mean it was some special occasion. Well, we'll have to see what we can find out about it."

"It isn't important, is it?"

"Every move he made that last week of his life is important," Jim told the young man.

He had no more questions for Dean. Very soon thereafter Elaine and he left and then Lieutenant Schmidt.

Margaret and Jim went to bed. The latter showed no

114

inclination to talk about the case while they were undressing. As soon as he was in bed he fell asleep. Margaret, who had a tendency toward insomnia, had long envied her husband his ability to shed his problems in sleep as soon as he was settled for the night.

She lay awake for about an hour wondering who had killed Leonard and when and why it had been done. His body being found at his cottage brought up the horrid possibility that someone here at the lake had killed him, someone she knew.

At the very end of her wakeful period Margaret found her thoughts turning to Elaine. Having her next door, and seeing her every day for the past ten days, hadn't changed her first impression of the younger woman. She wasn't ever going to like Elaine.

She was lovely looking though, Margaret told herself, and she had faultless taste in clothes. Quite expensive taste, too, for the wife of a young man who hadn't yet established himself. Extravagance could be chalked up against her; it might be one of the reasons Dean wasn't farther ahead financially. His fatuous attitude toward her would lead him into condoning every spendthrift thing she did. He not only condoned, he collaborated. For instance, the new charm on Elaine's bracelet must have cost fifty or sixty dollars. He couldn't afford to buy his wife that kind of a present. But he would do anything, it seemed, in trying to make her happy.

This was Margaret's last thought. She went to sleep on it.

Ten

The next morning while Margaret prepared an early breakfast Jim got on the telephone. He talked with Goodrich, the state's attorney, who said he would plan to be at his office at eight that morning to confer with Jim. Then he called the Hampton Police Department to clear through it a request to the state police Identification Bureau to make an examination of Leonard Riggott's apartment.

By that time Margaret had breakfast ready. While he ate Jim glanced at the front page of the morning paper. The finding of Leonard's body commanded large headlines, and in the story itself there was more than one reference to the possibility of foul play, but the word murder did not actually appear.

At seven-thirty the county detective was on his way to Hampton. At eight o'clock he was in the state's attorney's office, filling in for Goodrich the outline of the case he had given him on the telephone the night before.

"A man like Riggott, it sounds like money or

women," Goodrich commented at the end. "I suppose you'll go to his bank as soon as it opens."

"Yes, and I'd better have a written statement from you authorizing me to look into his affairs. You know how banks are."

"We want to find out right away the provisions of his will," Goodrich continued, when he had written the authorization and handed it to the county detective. "According to the nephew, the bank's the executor. With the story that's in the paper this morning, they won't lose any time getting the will over to probate court, and the judge won't lose any time opening it. I don't think they'll object to having you present when it is opened."

"I hope not," Jim said, remembering occasions in the past when banks had been, from his point of view, purely obstructionist. "There's also a safe-deposit box that will have to be opened. I have the key to it along with his other keys. Then he has a safe at his apartment. The nephew said he didn't keep much in it, but it'll have to be opened just the same."

"Yes, it will. Cobb and Bailo are going ahead questioning the rest of the tenants at the apartment house today?"

"They'll keep at it."

"It's not going to do much good to ask people about things that happened over two months ago," Goodrich remarked complainingly. "I don't like this kind of a case."

"Neither do I." Jim looked at his watch and got to his feet. "I'd better get a move on," he said. "It's quarter of nine and I want to be on the bank's doorstep when they open this morning."

"See you later," Goodrich said, and settled back to look at his mail.

Jenny, Jim's secretary, had arrived and had a phone call for him to take when he came out of the state's attorney's office.

He took it in his own office. Cobb was on the line. He said, "We talked to one more of the tenants after I called you last night. A Mrs. Streicher who lives across the hall from Mrs. Madler. Her and Mrs. Madler are on the outs so she gave us an earful. She said one day she was there when Mrs. Madler was supposed to have lunch with Riggott. He didn't show up, he sent some flowers instead and Mrs. Madler blew her stack. She said he couldn't treat her like that and get away with it. She'd fix him good, she said."

Jim foresaw difficult moments ahead with Loretta. She could have been making an angry, meaningless threat, but still it would have to be investigated. He inquired, "You sure this Mrs. Streicher wasn't just being vindictive because they're on the outs?"

"How can you ever be sure of anything when you're dealing with women?" Cobb demanded.

"Well, what else did she say?"

"She said Riggott used to be at Mrs. Madler's till all hours of the night and that they weren't just holding hands either."

"You'd better talk to her again today," Jim suggested.

"Yeah. Right now I'm at the apartment house and Bailo's gone to see the garage attendants. The superintendent's wife just gave me the name of a new flame of Riggott's. She took a message from her on the phone for him. Her name is Mrs. Dorothy Lanford and he lives on Lee Boulevard. You want me to take a run out and see her?"

"I guess you'd better stay where you are for now," Jim said, knowing that Cobb's approach to the opposite sex was notably lacking in finesse. "I'll try to see Mrs. Lanford myself later today."

He hung up and at once he had another call. This one was from Lieutenant Hildreth who said, "Well, you certainly got yourself a package."

"Haven't I though."

They talked about the case, Jim keeping it brief, saying, "I'm just leaving for Riggott's bank. They're the executors of his estate."

"Anything I can do for you?"

"Yes, there is. I'd like to get a line on a Mrs. Dorothy Lanford who lives on Lee Boulevard. She's supposed to have been a girl friend of Riggott's. I doubt she'd be in your files—he'd hardly go for anyone with a police record—but I would appreciate whatever you can pick up on her fairly fast. I want to talk to her later today."

"I'll see what I can do," Hildreth said. "You got a real case there. I'm glad it isn't mine."

"Don't be too sure it isn't," Jim advised him. "The body was moved after death, but we don't know yet where death took place. Maybe the Bureau people will find something in his apartment that shows he was killed there."

"To hell with you," Hildreth said. "Don't try to dump it on me."

"Why not?" Jim asked as he hung up.

Immediately he dialed the hospital number. He didn't expect a report on the autopsy so soon, but it wouldn't hurt to remind Eisenberg that he was waiting for it.

When he was connected with the pathologist he said, "O'Neill speaking. How you coming?"

"My God, man, I'm just getting started," Eisenberg protested. "You sit on a body for two months and then you want an autopsy report in two minutes. Give me a little time."

"How much time?"

"Well, unless a toxicological is required, I may have something for you in a couple of hours."

"All right, I'll call you back in two hours," Jim said.

"I know you will. You always do."

It was nine o'clock when Jim finished talking with the pathologist. He left his office quickly before another call could come in to delay him. Even so, he wasn't going to be on the bank's doorstep when it opened.

Arriving there, he found that the bank officials were ready to take action on Riggott's estate. A vice-president read Goodrich's request for co-operation, seated Jim beside his desk, and rang for the ledger card of the account. While they waited for it to be brought to them Jim introduced the matter of the safe-deposit box, saying he had the key to it.

The vice-president looked doubtful. Jim said flatly, "This seems to be a murder case. The faster we get information on Riggott the better."

The vice-president said, "Excuse me," and went away to consult someone else, the president or the chairman of the board or, thought Jim, maybe even the state banking commissioner.

However, after his return things moved rapidly. The ledger card of Riggott's account was laid before the county detective and a copy of Riggott's will. The vice-president said the judge of probate had been called and, in view of the circumstances, he had given his consent to having the safe-deposit box opened by one of his representatives with an officer of the bank and Jim present. Also, he had authorized the bank to give Jim a copy of the will.

Jim glanced through it. Just as Glenn Saxton had said, he received half his uncle's estate and the other half went to Hampton General Hospital.

The ledger card of the checking account appeared to be a record of normal expenditures. When the county detective asked about seeing the checks themselves, he was taken to a room in the depths of the bank and here pictures of all the checks the dead man had written since the first of the year were run on a screen for him. None of them, through its amount or its payee, pointed at blackmail or any sort of dubious financial transaction.

By the time Jim had seen the checks the probate-court representative had arrived. Jim produced the key to the safe-deposit box. He and the vice-president sat down in a room off the vault to look on while the probate-court man spread the contents of the box out on a table in front of him. Among them was a notebook that listed all of Leonard Riggott's holdings except for the forty shares of Atlantic Telephone and Telegraph Company stock he had bought not long before his death.

They didn't know yet about the Atlantic stock. They checked and rechecked bonds and stock certificates against the notations in the book. The thirty-two government bonds Dean had stolen were listed. When they couldn't find them Jim said, "There's a safe at his apartment. Maybe he kept the bonds there."

A call to Tad confirmed this; he said Leonard had kept the bonds in his safe.

The combination of the safe was also listed in the invaluable notebook and a call to the probate judge elicited his permission to open it.

It was past noon. Before they left the bank to go to the apartment, Jim phoned Dr. Eisenberg.

The latter said, "Well, I've been waiting to hear from you. He was killed by a bullet from a small-caliber gun, a .22 I would say. I have the bullet and it's in good condition. From the course it took and the spot where it lodged itself, I'd say it was fired from a distance of two to three feet. It penetrated the chest in the left fifth intercostal space, passing through the heart, and lodging itself in the seventh thoracic vertebra."

"In other words, it lodged in his spine?"

"That's right. The lab has his clothes, I suppose?"

"Yes."

"Well, they won't find any powder burns on them. So," the pathologist concluded briskly, "it looks like you got yourself a murder case."

"I knew that before I called you."

"Now you've got my seal on it—I'll send the bullet along to the lab."

"Thanks," Jim said. He hung up and called the state's attorney to tell him what he had learned from Eisenberg. Then he called Lieutenant Schmidt. The latter wasn't at the Garfield Barracks. Jim left a message for him regarding the autopsy findings.

On the way to Leonard's apartment, Jim stopped at a restaurant and bought lunch for the vice-president and the probate man. He felt benevolent toward them. They were cooperating with him and it was, he felt, only fair that in return Hampton County should pay for their lunch.

The technicians from the Identification Bureau were still at work in the apartment when they arrived, but the den, Jim was told, was all his; they had finished their examination of it. The few prints he had found in it, the fingerprint man said, were probably going to be the maid's or Riggott's. They were in out-of-the-way places. All the obvious surfaces appeared to have been dusted and polished regularly.

Jim opened the safe. In an envelope in one of the compartments were the traveler's checks Riggott had bought at the bank on Thursday, April 22. In another compartment were insurance policies and various miscellaneous papers.

The county detective located the key to the safe drawer in Riggott's desk. He unlocked it, found the passport inside and nothing else.

He called Tad again. The broker said no, he didn't think Leonard had sold his government bonds; they were still on Tad's list of his holdings. "Of course he could have sold them without my knowledge," Tad added. "But I don't see why he would. As far as I know, I handled all his buying and selling."

"We'll be right down to look your list over," Jim told him.

Tad had his list ready for their inspection when they arrived at Beecher's. They compared it item by item with the listings in the notebook, which the probate man had taken in charge. On Tad's list was included the forty shares of Atlantic stock purchased in early April.

The probate man looked at Jim. "The certificate wasn't in his box."

"It's probably in his safe," Tad said helpfully. "Whenever he bought stock he'd put it there until he got around to taking it to the bank."

"We've opened his safe," Jim said. "Neither the stock certificate nor the government bonds are in it."

"They're—not?"

"No, they're not."

Tad, his round face pale under its tan, was silent, absorbing the shock of the county detective's revelation. At last he said with a weak smile, "I was his broker. I think my books had better be audited—and my personal finances investigated too." His gaze settled on Jim. "You can have my income tax records, my own investment sheet, my bankbooks, everything. I won't have a moment's peace of mind until they've been examined."

"Okay," Jim said. "I'd feel the same way if I were in your place." He wanted to add something that would be reassuring to Tad in his distress, but there was nothing he could say.

It was three o'clock when he drove his companions back to the bank. He told the probate man about Riggott's mail at the post office and added, "I'll be busy the rest of the afternoon, but I'd appreciate it if you'd let us have someone else from the state's attorney's office present while you're opening it."

"Well, Judge Thornton hasn't objected to anything you've done so far," the probate man replied, "and I don't see why he'd object to that. If he's going to open it today."

Jim said patiently, "In a murder case we don't know

what may be of value to us. There may be information in that mail that we can use. Will you explain that to Judge Thornton? I'm sure he'll see how important it is to open it right away. I'll send someone along to his office."

"All right," the probate man said. "I'll talk to him about it."

Jim watched the vice-president and the probate man as they got out of his car and walked toward the bank. They put their heads together to talk. They were having themselves a high old time, he reflected. This was probably the closest contact they had ever had with a murder.

He drove to his office. Goodrich wasn't there, but Cobb was just reporting in, prepared to settle down and discuss the total lack of information his day had produced.

Jim said, "You can tell me about it later," and sent him along to probate court to sit in on the opening of Leonard Riggott's mail.

He himself sat down at his desk and reached for his telephone. He called Lieutenant Hildreth, brought him up to date on developments, and asked, "What did you find out about Mrs. Dorothy Lanford?"

"Nothing questionable," the lieutenant replied. "She's a widow in her late thirties, husband died from cancer two years ago. She has a son, who's away at college, and enough dough to maintain a nice home. She drives a '52 Nash, belongs to a couple of women's clubs, has a good credit rating, and, generally speaking, a good reputation."

"Well, I guess I'll take a run out to see her," Jim said.

As soon as he hung up a call came in for him from

Lieutenant Schmidt who told him he was just back from the lake and that a search of the cottage and grounds, the boathouse, and adjoining wood had turned up nothing that seemed to have any bearing on the murder.

He had two men out now, he said, asking questions at the farmhouses in the vicinity. He had just talked with the Garfield constable who was making intensive inquiries in the village. But, he added, he didn't expect any results. Two months was a long time.

"Yes indeed," said Jim, who suspected that before the case was closed he was going to become very tired of that remark.

He gave Schmidt a résumé of his own activities during the day and said he would call him when he got out to the lake that night.

He was ready to set out for Mrs. Lanford's, but before he could leave he had another call. He picked up the receiver and said, "O'Neill speaking."

"Oh, Mr. O'Neill . . ." It was a woman's voice, light and reedy, hesitant in tone. "I'm calling about Leonard Riggott's death."

"Yes? What is your name, please?"

"Mrs. Dorothy Lanford."

She couldn't see the way Jim's mouth quirked in surprise. She went on, "I was a friend of his and I was so shocked and grieved this morning to read about his death."

"I'm sure all his friends were." Jim spoke with due sympathy.

"I've been trying to make up my mind to call you," she continued. "From what the paper said it seems he must have died around April 24. I thought you might

126

want to know I saw him the twenty-second and we were to have had dinner together the twenty-fourth— but he didn't come and I didn't hear from him—it was my birthday, you see, and the dinner was planned as sort of a little celebration—" She was close to tears. "When I think of it, it seems so dreadful—"

"May I run out and talk it over with you, Mrs. Lanford?"

"Yes, I guess that would be better." Her voice steadied. "I live at 114 Lee Boulevard. It's a white house with blue shutters just past the corner of Edgewood Street."

"I'll be right out, Mrs. Lanford. Thank you for calling."

Jim stopped at Jenny's desk to tell her where he was going. He said he'd be back when he left Mrs. Lanford's and if Cobb or Bailo came in he wanted them to wait to see him.

Ten minutes later the county detective was getting out of his car in front of the white house with blue shutters on Lee Boulevard.

Mrs. Lanford, small and slender, with hair too blond to be true and a pretty face that was still—with the aid of make-up skillfully applied—holding back the years, answered his ring at her door and led him into the living room. He sat down in the chair she indicated after she had settled herself on a sofa facing him. Her brown eyes showed traces of tears. She dabbed at them with a handkerchief and gave him a tremulous smile.

"I've been upset all day over poor Len," she said. "I hope I never have such a shock again as I had at breakfast this morning when I unfolded the paper and there was Len's picture and that frightful story . . ."

Jim had to listen to details of her reactions, what she had felt, what she had thought, what she had said—to herself, she explained, since she lived alone while her son was away at college—and how long it had taken her to make up her mind to call Jim.

His lean dark face wore its most attentive look. He expressed commiseration.

"Just think," she concluded finally, "when he didn't arrive to take me out on my birthday and I kept calling his number without getting an answer, I felt so bitter toward him. And all the while—" She broke off with a sob.

"Let's go back to the beginning, Mrs. Lanford," the county detective interposed. "When and where you met Mr. Riggott, and so forth."

She wiped away tears, sighed deeply, and replied, "I met him at a dance on Washington's Birthday at the golf club. We danced together several times and really did enjoy each other's company. Len was lots of fun—but you knew him yourself, didn't you? The paper said your cottage was next door to his at the lake."

"Yes. My wife and I knew him as a neighbor there."

"Then I don't have to tell you how much fun he was and what a delightful sense of humor he had."

Jim nodded although he wouldn't have described the dead man as having a delightful sense of humor and being lots of fun. But then, he hadn't found Leonard particularly congenial in any sense. His feelings toward him had probably been colored by Margaret's pronouncement that she couldn't stand professional lady-killers and that Leonard Riggott was a particularly self-satisfied example of the species.

He asked Mrs. Lanford if she had ever gone to

Leonard's cottage with him. No, she said; he had mentioned it, though, and told her he would take her there when summer came.

She went on, "A few days after I met him at the dance he phoned and asked me to go to the theater with him. I went and had such a pleasant evening. That was the real beginning of our acquaintance . . ."

Mrs. Lanford paused to give Jim a sad earnest glance. "We got along very well together right from the start. We seemed to have so much in common."

She was off again. He had to sit through a reliving of the happy hours she had spent with Leonard, where they had gone, what they had done, the leaps and bounds by which their friendship had grown. She cried during the recital saying, "To think that it's all over— that I'll never see him again, never see that gay smile of his—"

Women, Jim reflected, his hazel eyes fixed on her, his facial muscles feeling the strain of remaining set in a sympathetic expression.

At last she brought them to April 22. They'd gone to the Atheneum that evening, she said, to a concert given by the Hampton Symphony Orchestra. Leonard subscribed to the series. He was so civic-minded. He had subscribed to all of Hampton's worthy causes. There was considerable depth to Leonard's outlook on life although it didn't always show. On the surface he seemed to be just another man about town who possessed sufficient means to indulge his every whim. But underneath, Mrs. Lanford assured Jim, Leonard wasn't really like that. He was serious. She was serious too. That was why their friendship had made such rapid strides. "And although," she interjected, "it was still only a friendship, I do feel that if Leonard had lived, we might have—well, he appreciated the fact that I had certain qualities he looked for in a woman—and from things he said, I feel that living alone was beginning to pall on him—and that if he'd lived, we might have—"

"You couldn't be more wrong," Jim said to himself, while aloud he made sounds of agreement that for her Leonard Riggott would eventually have given up his bachelor freedom. "I bet this room wouldn't hold all the women he took in with that line," he thought next.

She talked some more about how much Leonard had appreciated her serious, sensitive side: her interest in books and music and in long profound conversations about the meaning and purpose of life.

The longer she talked the more Jim became convinced that her association with Riggott had been as platonic as she implied. The dead man had been taking his time. He probably enjoyed the pursuit, the employment of various approaches, as much as he enjoyed the conquest itself when it was finally accomplished.

At last the county detective cut in on her. "Now, Mrs. Lanford, about that dinner date on April 24—it was your birthday, you said?"

"Yes. Leonard asked me to have dinner with him that night. He wouldn't tell me where we were going. Out of town, he said. It was to be a surprise. And now I'll never know—"

Tears threatened to overcome her. She couldn't be hurried. She dabbed at her eyes again and shifted her position and smoothed her skirt. Then, with a woebegone expression, she resumed, "He was to have

130

called for me at six-thirty that night. I was dressed and ready and he didn't come. I began to be worried. He'd never kept me waiting before. At seven-thirty I called him. His phone rang and rang, but he didn't answer. By eight-thirty I knew he wasn't coming. I'd called him twice in the meantime. I thought he'd had an accident on the way over and I wanted to contact the police or the hospitals, but I just didn't do it. I made myself some coffee and a sandwich. It must have been ten o'clock by that time . . .

"The first thing Sunday morning I went downstairs for the paper. I really expected to read that Leonard had been injured or killed in some sort of accident. But there wasn't a word about him. I looked through every page . . ."

She went on, "Then I felt I had a right to be annoyed. It was only about eight o'clock, but I went straight to the phone and called him. After the way he'd treated me I didn't care if I did get him out of bed. But again there was no answer . . .

"I tried his number three or four times that day. I tried it the next day too. There was never any answer.

"Then I remembered he'd been planning to go to Vancouver on a fishing trip. I thought perhaps he'd left earlier than he intended and had been in such a rush getting away he hadn't found time to phone me. All that week I expected a letter or a wire or even a long-distance call from him. I didn't hear from him, though, and it's bothered me ever since. There was no reason, you see, for him to drop me like that. Two nights before when he took me to the concert he was just as attentive as ever. We didn't quarrel, there was no way to account for what he'd done. Now, of course, I know what

131

happened. He was dead before six-thirty the night of my birthday. Otherwise he would have come."

Mrs. Lanford said this almost with satisfaction. Her wounded ego was healed at last. It was his own death, nothing less, that had kept Leonard away from her.

Jim, without taking into consideration the irresistible nature of Mrs. Lanford's appeal, reached the same conclusion as hers: Leonard had been dead by six-thirty on April 24. Her story was supported by every other piece of information he had been able to gather concerning the dead man's activities on that date.

He asked his standard question about whether or not she had noticed any signs of worry in Leonard's attitude the last few times she saw him, especially on April 22.

Mrs. Lanford shook her overly blond head. She had noticed nothing like that.

It was the only answer he was ever going to get, Jim felt. Whatever lay behind Riggott's death—and he must ahead of time have had some knowledge of its motive—he had kept it to himself. He and his murderer had kept it to themselves.

After listening a little longer to Mrs. Lanford's sorrowful review of the rare qualities of Leonard's personality, the perfect rapport that had existed between them, Jim was able to ease his way out of the house. He thanked her for calling him, telling her it was too bad everyone didn't have her sense of duty in helping the police, not telling her he had been on his way to see her when her call came in.

She stood in the doorway until he had driven away and turned back into her house with renewed confidence in herself. The sense of failing charms and masculine rejection that had harassed her since the night Leonard vanished from her life was gone. However shocked she might be by the knowledge he was dead, at least she could feel assured he had not lost interest in her. And she hadn't, after all, known him very long. In a little while she would be ready to renew her quest for a second husband. In the meantime, in her circle, she would be the heroine of a tragedy. She went to the phone to call her dearest friend and tell her about Jim's visit.

He was a most attractive man himself, Mrs. Lanford thought, as she dialed the number. Not at all like the picture she'd formed of detectives. It was a pity he was married . . .

Jim returned to his office. Cobb was waiting for him with the information that the dead man's mail had offered no clue to the reason for his murder. Bailo came in and reported that his day's work had yielded nothing of consequence.

The county detective gave them fresh assignments. Cobb was to start an investigation of Mrs. Lanford; Bailo was to go to the Hampton Club to see what he could learn from the members and the staff.

When they left, Jim was the only person remaining at the state's attorney's office. He picked up the telephone receiver and dialed Goodrich's home number to give him another report on the day's activities.

"I'm going to the lake now," he added. "I'll see Schmidt after dinner."

He went out to his car and headed for home.

Eleven

Sarah and Loria came in their usual hurtling rush to greet him when he drove into his yard. Margaret wasn't far behind them laughing as she said, "Here we are all lined up waiting our turn for hugs and kisses."

But the children weren't waiting. They hung on him vying for his attention, Sarah telling him how many times she had dived off the dock today, Loria about the picture of Juney and Rex she had drawn, while Jim kept exclaiming, "Hey, take it easy. One at a time."

"I'm woman-ridden," he declared, reaching out an arm to draw Margaret close. "That's what's the matter with me."

"Sure," she said, kissing the lobe of his ear. "You have a terrible life."

He showed himself duly impressed with Sarah's diving achievements, he praised Loria's drawing, disputing Sarah's scornful comments that it was all lopsided and didn't look a bit like their cat and dog anyway. At last the children returned to their own pursuits and in the blessed silence that ensued

Margaret and he went indoors.

"I've fed them already," she said. "They were starved."

"So am I. What's for dinner?"

"I curried the leftover lamb; and there's corn on the cob and salad and pie."

"Well, bring it on," said Jim. "No, let's have a drink first." He went to the cabinet that held their liquor supply. "What'll you have?"

"Not a cocktail. Just rye and soda, I guess."

He mixed the drinks, handed one to her, and propped himself up against the sink with his. He remarked, "I'm surprised the kids weren't all excited over having the police around today."

"They weren't here. I took them to Warrenton right after breakfast and bought two crates of strawberries on the way. Sarah helped me hull them and we got them all in the freezer. It was after four by the time we got back here and the excitement was over. Tommy came down to the beach with us and tried to tell the girls about the policemen who'd been around, but they didn't pay any attention to him."

Margaret was transferring food from pans to serving dishes as she talked. Jim, his drink in one hand, helped her carry them into the dining room that was little more than an ell off the kitchen.

She finished her drink after they were seated at the table and said, "Nicky was over a little while ago. She was quite upset. Lieutenant Schmidt was at their place half the afternoon, she said, and took Glenn through his whole life history acting as if he thought he'd murdered his uncle."

"Why not? Glenn's the obvious suspect. He's going

135

to inherit a pile of dough, enough not to have to worry about money again for the rest of his life. What better motive could you ask than that?"

"Well—none, I suppose."

"For that matter, Nicky rates as a suspect herself. She's married to Glenn and she'll get her share of the money."

"But if they had nothing to do with the murder, it seems too bad they have to go through all this questioning and suspicion."

Jim, filling his plate, gave a snort of derision. "Save your sympathy for someone who needs it. As long as I was innocent, I'd be glad to go through a lot more than they'll have to if I knew there was two or three hundred thousand bucks coming to me at the end of it."

They ate in silence for a few minutes. Then Jim said, "Didn't you once mention Nicky saying Glenn was worried about losing his biggest account?"

"Hampton Electronics. Seems the president's daughter is going to marry a man who's with a big advertising agency in New York and Nicky said there were rumors that the new son-in-law would take over the account. It's the backbone of Glenn's agency, Nicky said. He couldn't get by without it."

"Oh," said Jim. "You didn't tell me all this before."

"I did, but you didn't listen." Margaret's tone was accusing. "I'm always telling you things I hear and half the time you don't listen."

"Well, it'll have to be looked into," Jim said. "I don't know, though. Len was a big stockholder. It ought to have weighed pretty well against the claims of the president's new son-in-law."

At the end of dinner while they were drinking iced

coffee, Margaret said reflectively, "The more I see of Elaine the sorrier I feel for Dean. He tries so hard to give her the things she wants—more than he can afford, I'm sure—and it's like pouring money down a drain. She'll never be satisfied. This afternoon when we got back from Warrenton she started telling me how lucky I am because you have a car supplied to you and I have the use of ours. She said she's tired of Dean's taking theirs all day and being without one herself. She's trying to talk him into getting her one. Just imagine!" Margaret was indignant. "He's barely made a start at Beecher's and she wants a car of her own."

"Where does she think he'd get the money?"

"Well, she said something about his having picked up a little extra money on the stock market. But don't mention it to Tad. She let it slip out, then she told me she wasn't supposed to breathe a word of it, Tad wouldn't approve."

"I shouldn't think so," Jim commented. "Dean won't last long with him if he starts playing the market. And if he is doing it, Elaine ought to have more sense than to tell you about it."

"I know. Poor Dean. He seems so nice and he's crazy about her and all she thinks of is what she can get out of him."

"He married her. His tough luck." Jim's tone dismissed the subject. He lit a cigarette and pushed his chair back from the table. "I'm going to make a couple of calls and then I'll go over and see Loretta."

"Lord," Margaret said. "I'll be an outcast around here before this case is finished. Everyone except Elaine is acting sort of wary of me already. Sometimes the lot of a policeman's wife is not a happy one."

"You'll live through it," Jim told her.

The telephone rang. Goodrich was calling. He had some free time later this evening, he said, and he thought he'd drive out to the Garfield Barracks; Jim and Schmidt and he could talk the case over.

"Okay," Jim said. "I'll call Schmidt. What time will you be there?"

"Around nine-thirty."

"I'll see you then." The county detective hung up and called the state police barracks. Schmidt said he thought the Garfield constable should be asked to sit in on the discussion. Jim agreed and cut the conversation short. Whatever the lieutenant had to say would keep until they saw each other.

He found Loretta reclining on her porch glider. Her arms were linked under her head, her full skirt fell about her in graceful folds showing the long lines of her body to advantage. She held her pose, pretending unawareness of his arrival, while he climbed the steps.

Any kind of pretense annoyed Jim; the motive behind this example annoyed him particularly. Loretta was posing for his benefit because he was a man. It made no difference to her that he was happily married, that he had come to see her as a detective investigating a murder. If he had been the milkman, the laundryman, the garbage man, she would have done the same thing.

Loretta turned her head when he rapped on the screen door. "Oh, hello. I didn't see you. Come in."

She sat up then, asked him to sit down, and added, "Can I get you a drink?"

"No thanks." He sat down.

She lit a cigarette and told him it seemed impossible

Leonard had been murdered. It was just too awful, she said.

She felt no genuine grief, Jim realized. She hadn't loved the dead man any more than her successor, Mrs. Lanford, had. Both of them had had their eyes on his money. When you got right down to it, Jim thought next, there was no one who was really grieving over Riggott.

It was pretty grim to have your life end like that. It meant that in what counted most, your relationship with other people, you had been a failure. But, now that he stopped to think about it, what else could Riggott have been? He'd lived for himself and his death couldn't be expected to leave a void in anyone's life.

That was the way things added up: two and two made four. A bachelor vaunting his freedom could, in the end, become as emotionally bankrupt as the most crabbed old maid although he wouldn't, like her, be regarded as an object of pity or ridicule. . . .

Jim was blunt in telling Loretta why he was there, what Mrs. Streicher had said.

Her dark eyes flashed anger. Ann Streicher was a horrible creature, she declared, a busybody, an unmitigated liar. There wasn't a word of truth in her story.

The county detective proceeded to break down this declaration by citing details Mrs. Streicher couldn't have made up, deleting the latter's statements to Cobb, but even so bringing out enough to fan the quarrel between the two women into a feud that must last until they were in their graves.

Eventually, as he wrung admission after admission

139

from her, Loretta was reduced to tears. "I didn't mean a word I said that morning," she sobbed. "I was so furious at Len I just said whatever came into my head. But I didn't mean it. You know how it is, Jim. When we're mad we all say things we don't mean."

Which was perfectly true, he reflected, eying her with veiled distaste. She had become Riggott's mistress in the hope of marrying him. She was bound to feel bitterness and resentment when he threw her over. There was nothing yet in the way of proof that she'd carried out the threats she'd made against him.

Proving anything except that Riggott had been murdered was going to be tough, the county detective told himself, as he walked back to his cottage from Loretta's.

So far the only evidence they had consisted of a bullet of .22 caliber. For motive the best bet at the moment seemed to be the missing government bonds. They might still be accounted for, however.

Tad was sitting on his back steps and said "Hi" as Jim walked past him, but made no effort to engage him in conversation as he would ordinarily. Jim remembered what Margaret had said about being an outcast. Well, he thought, it was no choice of his that a murder turned up on his very doorstep.

When they assembled at the police barracks that night Lieutenant Schmidt lined up chairs in his office for the three of them, the state's attorney, the Garfield constable, and Jim. He himself sat down behind his desk and said, "I've just had a call from the Identification Bureau. Riggott was shot with a .22 Iver-Johnson target pistol. There's no record of anyone we're investigating owning such a gun."

"At least we know what kind to look for," the constable said.

"I'm afraid it's at the bottom of some lake or river long ago," Schmidt told him. "We'll look for it though. We'll give it plenty of publicity."

He went on, "The Bureau says there were bits of fuzz from a khaki army blanket on Riggott's clothing. Apparently he was wrapped in one after he was shot."

"There are a lot of those blankets kicking around," Goodrich observed. "You can buy them almost anywhere."

"Yes," Schmidt agreed, but he knew, they all knew, they would have to try to trace that particular blanket. He added, "There were three or four hemlock needles caught in the sole of Riggott's shoe. Sergeant Crowley, who was brought up in Garfield and knows the country around here like the back of his hand, says there's a good-sized stand of hemlock on an old wood road a couple of miles above the lake, but there's none anywhere near the cottage. It's all oak and pine through there. He's going to look around the old road tomorrow and see what he can find."

Goodrich nodded. "If Riggott was killed in the woods, his body was wrapped in the army blanket and taken to the cottage later on. The woods would be a good place to commit murder. Even if the shot was heard, no one would notice it particularly."

"It would mean his murderer was someone he knew well and wasn't afraid of or he wouldn't have gone there with him," Jim said. "Then, after he was killed, his body would have been hidden in the trunk of the car. But when was it taken to the cottage? If he was killed April 24, it couldn't have been that day because

141

we were all at the lake cleaning up my place after the vandalism. The next day was Sunday and there'd be too many people around. If I'd been the murderer, I'd have waited until Monday."

"Where would you keep the body in the meantime?" the constable inquired.

"I'd leave it in the trunk of my car and lay low over the week end. That would be the safest—" He broke off. "This is guesswork. We'd better go back to what facts we have."

He reviewed for them what he had done that day. Schmidt then described the activities at the lake, his long fruitless questioning of Glenn Saxton.

"We'll have to go into the financial picture at that agency of his right away," Goodrich said.

"There's a new angle on it." Jim told them about the Hampton Electronics account. They talked it over. As things stood, Glenn, with the most to gain from the murder, was their chief suspect. But the others at the lake, the Beechers and Loretta Madler, also came under discussion. Dean Lipscomb was mentioned only incidentally as working for Tad and having had a casual acquaintance with Leonard Riggott.

They went on to discuss the many factors that pointed to April 24 as the date of death. Jim said, "It looks as if we can assume that on that date he was killed between eight-thirty in the morning when he talked to Lieutenant Schmidt and six-thirty that evening when he was due at Mrs. Lanford's."

Even Goodrich, with his lawyer's caution about assumptions, was ready to concede that for the present, at least, they could accept Jim's.

The constable said, "Maybe you don't have to allow

that much margin. The nephew said he couldn't get him on the phone when he got home from the lake that afternoon."

"But we can't accept anything he says as evidence until he's cleared of suspicion himself," Jim reminded him.

"Oh, that's right." The constable turned red with embarrassment. In trying to make a useful suggestion, he had shown himself up in front of these professionals as a small-town cop who needed to have the most obvious point spelled out for him. He retreated into silence. He wouldn't say another word, he promised himself.

"There's another assumption—or indication, rather—we should bear in mind," Schmidt remarked. "The whole thing shows so much familiarity with the setup at the lake that it keeps you thinking about the people right in that little group of yours, Mr. O'Neill."

"I know," Jim said. "I hope you're wrong."

Goodrich brought up the missing holdings. "The bonds were government threes payable to bearer, but the stock certificate was made out to Riggott. I suppose, though, on the black market . . ." His voice fell away regaining body as he added, "Of course we don't know yet that they were stolen. We'll have to see what the Atlantic records show. The bonds are tougher. I had a talk with the probate judge about them tonight. It seems Riggott inherited them from his father and there's no record of the serial numbers. There is the possibility that Riggott sold them, not through Beecher, but through some other broker or a bank."

Jim offered no comment. He foresaw the work

ahead, inquiries from broker to broker and bank to bank, trying to locate the bonds.

The conversation turned to the people who had been at the lake on April 24 and their fragmentary recollections of what they had done that day after they arrived back in Hampton. They weren't, any of them, able to produce proof that they hadn't gone to see Leonard; but the police weren't able to produce proof that they had.

Jim said, "I've been thinking about the call from Riggott and the vandalism at my cottage the same night. It kept me away from my office the next day after I told him I'd be there if he wanted to see me. He knew I was going to be tied up at the lake the whole day; the lieutenant had mentioned it to him."

Schmidt eyed him with sudden alertness. "Phony vandalism?"

"That's what I'm wondering. To draw me off. No real damage was done."

"Then Riggott made a trip to the lake to see you."

"Let's say he might have started out on one and was murdered en route."

"That would bring the thing still closer to your lake neighbors," the lieutenant pointed out.

"Yes. It's occurred to me that no outsider would even know for sure which cottage belonged to me. There's no name plate or anything to identify it."

"Mailbox?" Goodrich asked.

"They're all in a row on the highway at the end of the lake road."

"And the supposed vandals, the teen-age boys, were never caught?"

"And no repetition of the vandalism," Schmidt

supplied. "If it had been genuine, I'd have expected it to continue. Which brings us to the call from the anonymous motorist. If Mr. O'Neill's theory is right, the call was made by the murderer and was as phony as the vandalism."

"And," said Jim, "it all but pins the murder on one of the people at the lake."

On this there was general agreement.

While the conference at the police barracks was still in progress Elaine and Dean were in their room at the Beecher cottage. She was already in bed reading while he was getting undressed. At last she laid aside her book and said, "Well, having the police around today provided a change. This place is deadly dull most of the time."

"It's better than being in that hot apartment in town," Dean reminded her defensively.

"I don't know that it is. There I could at least get out and go somewhere. Here I'm stranded. Mrs. Beecher seems satisfied to sit here all day; she doesn't care about having a car; she doesn't even know how to drive. But I'd like to be able to do something once in a while. I'd like to play golf, for instance. I suggested it to Margaret O'Neill and she said she'd take me some day soon when she could make plans for the children. But now, I suppose, with this murder thing going on, she won't get around to it."

Elaine's tone was eloquent of discontent. She looked at Dean reproachfully. "I still don't understand why you can't ever ride in with Mr. Beecher and leave our car here for me."

He sat down on the side of the bed and looked at her. In her sheer nightgown, her hair loose on the pillow, he had only to look at her to have his senses quicken. His hand went out to stroke her arm. He sought response from her tonight. He had been on edge since the discovery of the body. He could and did tell himself over and over that he had nothing to fear, but these assurances seemed to have no effect on his tight nerves. He wanted Elaine. He wanted to lose himself in making love to her tonight.

She drew her arm away repeating, "I still don't understand why—"

"Look, darling"—he tried to speak patiently—"you know Tad does a lot for me, that they've both been very generous. But we can't impose too much. And it would be an imposition to ask him to take me back and forth from here. He's the boss at Beecher's and free to set his own hours. I'm not, though. I have to stay there until five o'clock. I can't ever expect Tad to tie himself down to waiting for me."

She didn't answer. She looked past him. He said on a coaxing note, "Elaine, please try to see it my way."

"Well . . ." She sat up in bed and gave him an eager smile. "Dean, that money you made on the market—no matter what you say, I just know you've got some of it left. Enough to buy me a car. Oh, not a new car," she went on quickly to forestall his protest. "Anything at all would do. Just so I needn't be stuck without one, day after day. It would make such a difference to me, Dean . . ."

Her arms went around his neck, she made herself a soft warm weight against him. "I do get bored; you know what it's like, Mrs. Beecher old enough to be my

146

mother and there's only Margaret and Nicky to fall back on and they're wrapped up in their children and don't seem to need any outside recreation. I don't know what to do with myself half the time. If I had a car of my own, though—"

"But being out here at the lake is only temporary," Dean replied. "We'll be back in town in another week or two and there you're right on a bus line and can—"

"Bus line!" She drew away from him, her voice sharp with displeasure. "You use it. I want a car. I don't care what it is as long as I have one."

Dean knew better than to say yes. He knew that right now, of all times, he shouldn't buy Elaine a car. The police would discover the theft of the bonds and would be watching for signs of affluence in anyone who had the least connection with Leonard Riggott.

But Elaine put her arms around him again and murmured, "Please, Dean, please say you'll do something about getting a car for me."

He kissed her bare shoulder. He said, "We'll see," and then, before he lost all sense of caution in her embrace, he added, "But not while we're staying with the Beechers. We mustn't let him think we're extravagant."

"Oh Dean," she said, her arms tightening around him. "You can be so sweet when you want to."

Twelve

Leonard Riggott was buried at the beginning of July. By the end of the month the solution to his murder seemed as far away as ever to Jim in spite of the work he had done on the case.

Lieutenant Schmidt had worked as hard as he, scouring the woods in the vicinity of Garfield wherever hemlock was found, questioning every villager who had known the dead man, and even dragging the lake in front of Riggott's cottage on the chance that if the gun had been thrown into it from the dock he might find it.

Jim had worked from the Hampton end, questioning innumerable friends and acquaintances of Riggott's. He had gone back to Mrs. Lanford in the hope of jogging further information out of her. He had held many sessions with Glenn Saxton. Cobb and Bailo and he had made the tedious round of banks and brokers trying to trace a legitimate disposal of the missing bonds, going on with it even after they learned from Atlantic that its records showed no transfer of ownership of the forty shares of company stock

Leonard had bought.

Tad's books had been audited, his personal finances scrutinized. All his affairs were found to be in good order. Glenn's advertising agency had been thoroughly investigated and, though small, it seemed sound. Glenn deprecated the possibility of losing his biggest account, Hampton Electronics. "I've still got it," he said, "and I was counting on Uncle Len's influence to keep it for me."

Loretta Madler, they learned, lived on alimony. Her checking account showed deposits of five hundred a month and no more. There were no extra sums credited to it before or after the murder.

Dean Lipscomb's account received some attention from Jim. His balance was two or three hundreds above what the county detective expected it to be, but not large enough to center his attention on it.

In response to the publicity they had given the murder gun they had received a flood of information that covered everything from Civil War Colts to World War II Lugers but not the Iver-Johnson they were looking for.

Jim and Cobb were sitting in the former's office on a hot, sticky afternoon early in August discussing their lack of progress, Jim behind his desk, Cobb stretched out in a big leather armchair facing him.

"I've got to get this thing cleared up before my vacation," the county detective announced. His vacation, scheduled for the last two weeks of August, was very much on his mind these days. Margaret and he were planning to leave the children with her mother and to take a trip to the Gaspé Peninsula.

"I don't know how you're going to do it," Cobb said.

Jim didn't know either. He was silent.

"I just hope I never have to walk into another bank," Cobb remarked presently. He shook his head. "After what I been through this past month. I'm allergic to banks."

Jim, sunk in lethargy, made no reply. When he spoke again he was musing aloud. "Beecher, Saxton, Loretta Madler . . . they were all so eager to open their safe-deposit boxes for me . . . brings up the question of another box under an assumed name."

Cobb eyed him suspiciously. "You're not thinking— look, you'd never be able to trace it and even if you could you'd have to have some real evidence to show the bonds were in it before you could get a court order to open it. You might as well forget that angle."

"I don't know." Jim slumped lower in his chair, lit a cigarette he didn't want, and ran his hand around the inside of his damp, loosened collar. He wished he was at the lake, in swimming with Margaret and the children.

He said, "The stock certificate and the bonds were stolen by the murderer. At least we can be sure of that after our month's work. And I'm pretty much convinced the theft came first and brought on the murder."

His shirt was sticking to the back of his chair. He shifted his position and continued, "I think Riggott called me the day before he was killed because he'd discovered the theft, knew who was responsible for it, and didn't want to take it right to the police. Which means it was someone he was friendly with."

Cobb did not comment. Jim was repeating himself. They had talked over his theory many times during the past month without ever coming any closer to the identity of the thief and murderer.

"And then that phony vandalism at my place," Jim went on. "Drawing me away from my office, setting the stage for Riggott to drive to the lake with his murderer to see me—"

Jim broke off. He knew he had said all of it before, each time emphasizing the point that the dead man had known his murderer well enough to give no thought to being in danger from him.

Cobb's answer was as fixed as Jim's statement. Invariably he said, "Riggott had holes in his head if he felt safe with anyone, no matter who it was, who'd stolen over thirty thousand bucks from him and knew he was trying to get it back."

He produced his answer again. "Holes in his head . . ."

They were reduced to repeating themselves because they had nothing new to say. Jim decided he'd had enough of it. The thing for him to do was to knock off for the day, go home to the lake, have a swim and then, when he felt cool and refreshed, sit down and concentrate on finding a brand-new approach to the murder.

He told Cobb what he meant to do. When he came to the new approach part of his program Cobb, although he had immense respect for Jim's abilities, looked skeptical. "You'll have to make like a magician," he declared. "Rabbits out of a hat."

"Sure," said Jim. "Another day another rabbit out of a hat."

He cleared his desk and started home.

Margaret and the children were alone in the colony

that day. The Beechers hadn't yet arrived from a long week end in New Hampshire, Loretta was also away, and Nicky had gone to Hampton in the morning with her husband and son. Margaret guessed at a visit to the dentist for Tommy whose baby teeth had been causing him trouble. She had to guess instead of having Nicky tell her because the younger woman was not as free as she had once been in telling Margaret about her affairs. Jim's investigation of the murder had placed the O'Neills in a difficult position with their neighbors at the lake.

After lunch Margaret settled Loria for her nap and got into a bathing suit. She paused before a full-length mirror for a pleased inspection of her figure, still slender and firm at thirty-seven, and then took Sarah down to the beach.

She brought a book with her and, after a swim, stretched out on a blanket with one eye on what she read and the other on her daughter, who was tirelessly practicing her diving.

The solitude was pleasant after yesterday, Sunday, when Jim and she had been obliged to entertain a horde of uninvited guests. Sarah came out of the water at last and vanished around in back of the cottage to busy herself with her frogs.

Margaret began to find the sun too hot and moved her blanket back into the shade. She had just made herself comfortable again when she heard a car coming along the lake road. She looked around saying to herself, "Oh lord, who will this be?"

It was Elaine Lipscomb driving a Chevrolet convertible with the top down and braking to a stop at the edge of the beach.

"Why hello," Margaret said, sitting up and making her tone cordial. "This is a surprise."

Elaine slid out of the car. She was wearing a sleeveless sheath of green silk shantung. It was perfectly plain, but it fitted her very well and could rely on good lines for its effect. It looked expensive, Margaret thought, taking it in with one glance.

Elaine had her blond hair pinned high on her head and was carrying a waterproof bag, which held her bathing suit. She said, "It's frightfully hot in town. I knew Mrs. Beecher was away, but I decided to come out anyhow and impose on you for a swim."

"Well, fine," Margaret replied, getting to her feet. "Come on up to the cottage and put on your suit." She asked the question that was uppermost in her mind. "Your car?"

"Yes." Elaine was elaborately casual. "I told you I wanted one and Dean picked this one up for me the other day in Hampton. It's not new, of course—it's a '50—but it seems to have had good care and it was practically a giveaway, Dean says. He bought it from some Grimaldi character who deals in used cars and all it cost was six hundred and fifty."

"Six hundred and fifty?" Margaret walked up to the car for a closer view of it. It was in excellent condition and looked almost new. "That was a buy," she commented.

"Yes, wasn't Dean clever?" Elaine's tone revealed pride in her husband's accomplishment. "I'm so thrilled. It's the first time I've had a car of my own. Or rather," she added with a laugh, "one that will be mine when Dean gets it paid for."

Dean had won her approval by giving her what she

wanted most at the moment, Margaret reflected. He had better bask in it while it lasted; presently Elaine would set her heart on something else he couldn't afford.

While they walked up to the cottage and Elaine changed into her bathing suit Margaret's mind was on the car and what it stood for in the Lipscombs' relationship, her endless demands, his eagerness to please her at any cost.

At any cost. Margaret repeated the phrase to herself. Regardless of a lucky windfall from the stock market Dean wasn't in a position to maintain two cars. Elaine must realize it; yet she seemed unconcerned. She was still talking about her new car when they were on their way back to the beach. Then she looked down at her hand and stopped short. "Oh, my ring," she exclaimed. 'I don't want to wear it in the water."

Margaret glanced at it. "You'd better take it back to the cottage," she said. "You wouldn't want to lose a beautiful diamond like that."

"Indeed not. I've had it a long time." Elaine spoke hurriedly and added with emphasis, "A long, long time." She took off the ring and returned to the cottage with it.

Margaret, sitting down on the blanket in the shade, found Elaine's remark about the ring odd. Or was it only her manner in making it that was odd? No, it was the remark itself as well. She'd said she'd had it a long, long time. Well, then, it was her engagement ring. Why not say so instead of saying it as she had?

While she was pondering the matter Elaine rejoined her and Sarah came running toward them calling, "Hello, Mrs. Lipscomb. Wanna see me dive?" Margaret then dismissed it from her thoughts.

A little later Loria awoke from her nap and came out of the cottage pulling on her bathing trunks. The two women and the children went in the water together and splashed and swam and tossed a ball back and forth. Elaine was in a gay mood paying more attention to Sarah and Loria than she ever had before.

After they had gone back to the cottage and were dressed, Margaret and the children in shorts and jerseys, Elaine in the green silk shantung, Margaret made a pitcher of iced grape juice and served it with cake. As they grouped themselves on the porch Loria hung over Elaine, leaning on the arm of her chair, fascinated by Elaine's charm bracelet, wanting to spin the wheels of the car and turn the propeller blades of the airplane. Margaret said, "Loria, sit down, please. You mustn't hang over Mrs. Lipscomb like that."

She spoke too late. Loria's hand went out just then in an animated gesture and knocked the glass out of Elaine's hand. Grape juice spattered in all directions, but most of it ran into Elaine's lap.

She sprang to her feet with a cry of dismay and began to dab frantically with her paper napkin at the great wet purple patch on the silk shantung. Sarah ran for cloths, Margaret grabbed more napkins and held the dress out from Elaine trying to blot up the spreading stain. Loria stood back against the wall and burst into tears.

By the time Elaine had taken off the dress her face was stiff with anger. While Margaret sponged the stain Sarah took Elaine into the bedroom to find something of Margaret's to wear.

Loria had stopped crying before Elaine, in one of

Margaret's dresses, was ready to leave, but the child still looked crushed by the catastrophe she had brought about. Elaine's behavior made it plain that it was a catastrophe. She made no attempt to reassure Loria, nor would she hear of leaving the dress with Margaret.

"I prefer to take it with me," she said. "I bought it at Lansing's and I'll call them when I get home. They'll tell me if anything can be done with it."

Margaret walked out to the car with her, still apologizing for what had happened. "If it can be cleaned, please send the bill to me," she said. "If nothing can be done with it I want to replace it."

Elaine told her that wouldn't be necessary, but her tone belied her words. She added, "I'll have Dean give your dress to Mr. Beecher. I'm sure he won't mind bringing it back to you."

She drove away and didn't look back or wave as she swung her car around the bend out of sight.

Margaret stood looking after her. "What a bitch of a woman," she said aloud. "I feel sorrier than ever for Dean being married to her."

Seething, talking to herself, she walked back to the cottage. "If I'd been wearing a dress straight from Paris, I wouldn't have made that much fuss if something got spilled on it. She knew it was an accident and that Loria's only four years old. And I didn't even invite her out here. She came on her own. She's a perfect bitch. If the dress is ruined, I'm going to buy her another one. I'd buy it if it took the last cent I had. Maybe it will, coming from Lansing's, the prices they charge. What's she doing, anyway, buying dresses there?"

Margaret went into the cottage by the back door. As

she was crossing the living room to the front porch she heard Sarah say, "Hundreds of dollars probably. Hundreds and hundreds. All the money Daddy's got. Just think, he won't have any left."

"Sarah!" Margaret paused in the doorway and surveyed her daughters, Sarah in a chair, Loria huddled on a footstool. "Are you talking about that dress?"

"I was only telling Loria—she asked me if you'd have to buy Mrs. Lipscomb a new one—"

"Well, when she asks a question do you have to give her such a nonsensical answer?" Margaret's tone was crisp. She moved out on the porch and sat down midway between the two. "Let's not hear any more about hundreds and hundreds of dollars."

Loria eyed her mother with a gleam of hope. "It won't cost that much?"

"Of course not. But it will cost quite a bit. It's too bad, isn't it?" She looked at her younger daughter measuringly. "The next time we have guests do you think you'll remember what I've told you so many times—that you're not to hang over them or sit on the arms of their chairs or anything like that? It's not only annoying to them, it can lead to the kind of accident that happened today. If you'd remembered what Mommy's said to you about it, you wouldn't have been hanging on Mrs. Lipscomb and you wouldn't have spilled her drink on her dress."

Margaret's gaze went to Sarah who could, she thought, profit by being included in the rebuke. She said, "If both you girls will try to remember that I have a good reason for telling you not to do certain things, you'll stay out of a lot of trouble."

They looked subdued. She had lectured enough, she decided, and said, "Now I want you to tidy up the porch. Collect the glasses and plates and napkins on the tray and then you carry the tray to the kitchen, Sarah." Margaret stood up as she spoke. "I'd better take a look in the refrigerator. I don't know what I'm going to have for dinner tonight. Maybe we'll have to go to the village for something."

Her tone was deliberately matter-of-fact. It banished Elaine's dress, the whole incident.

The children hastened to do her bidding; this wasn't one of the times when they had to be prodded into action.

After the porch had been tidied Loria came out in the kitchen and pressed her head against her mother's thigh. "Could we have ice cream for dessert tonight?" she asked.

"Sure we can." Margaret gave her a hug. "I've got a quart of chocolate ripple in the freezer compartment."

"Goody goody gumdrops," Sarah exclaimed from the doorway. She went to her mother and pressed against her on the other side seeking a hug for herself.

While they stood there, Margaret with an arm around each of her daughters, they heard a car stop outside.

Sarah cocked her head. "Maybe it's Daddy."

"Not this early," Margaret told her, but Sarah broke away and Loria streaked after her to see who had arrived.

It was Jim. He was out of the car and Sarah was pouring out the story of Elaine's dress by the time Margaret reached them.

"What's this all about?" he inquired when he had

kissed her.

She laughed. "It seems as if you ought to be allowed to get inside the house at night before you're told about the day's disasters."

"Not around here," he said. "Not with this pair."

Giving him the details of what had happened, Margaret trailed after him into the bedroom where he pulled off his sticky clothes and put on swimming trunks. He said, "Well, if we have to buy her a dress, we have to buy it," and headed for the lake.

Margaret's inventory of the refrigerator had showed her she would have to go to the store. She left the children with Jim and drove to the village.

After dinner that evening he retreated to the porch with his notebook while Margaret washed the dishes with the children helping her.

He had a favorite porch chair, but Rex was already curled up in it. The dog thumped his tail so ingratiatingly and turned such a pleading look on Jim that the latter grinned and let him stay there, seating himself in another chair.

Juney, sauntering out on the porch in his wake, lacked his indulgent attitude. The chair Rex occupied was Juney's favorite too. The cat sat down to stare the dog out of countenance. Rex tried to pretend unawareness, closing one eye but watching out of the other. Rumbles of displeasure came from Juney's throat. He raised one paw in a tentative gesture that reminded Rex of the sharp claws that had raked his nose more than once.

The dog dared hold out no longer. He jumped off the chair and sought protection by draping himself across Jim's feet.

"Coward," said Jim. Then he said, "Maybe not, though. It's smart to know your own limitations."

Juney leaped gracefully into the vacated chair and settled down to have a good wash.

Jim opened his notebook.

When the dishes were finished the children went outdoors to play and Margaret joined her husband on the porch. A glance told her he was in one of his moods of deep concentration; the roof might fall in on him, a fire break out around his chair and he would not notice. She picked up a book and sat down near him. It was nearly eight o'clock. The Saxtons drove into their yard. They'd probably had dinner in town with Nicky's mother, Margaret reflected.

She tried to read, but her attention kept straying from her book. She heard the children's voices rising to a quarrelsome pitch in the back yard. She looked at Jim. He didn't even hear them. He was stretched out in a reclining chair, his dark brows knitted over the pages he was turning in his notebook.

Margaret went out to Sarah and Loria and brought them indoors. She supervised their preparations for bed and said, "Now you may go and kiss Daddy good night, but don't try to talk to him. He's working."

Daylight was fading when she went back on the porch after listening to the children's prayers. Jim was no longer studying his notes. He turned his head and said "Hi" as she seated herself.

"How's it going?" she ventured to ask.

"It isn't. I'm stymied."

"Oh." Her tone offered sympathy. It led him to add, "I'm going to keep on being stymied until I figure out what happened to those bonds. Everything centers around them."

He went on to tell her that none of the people he was investigating had cashed them or put them in their safe-deposit boxes. "So now," he concluded, "I'm faced with the prospect of a box or an account under an assumed name. And that would be a lulu to trace."

"How many banks are there in Hampton?"

"Counting the branch and suburban banks there are forty-six. It's meant a lot of checking."

Margaret murmured assent. Then she inquired, "How could you hope to pick out an assumed name out of thousands and thousands of depositors?"

"You'd begin with safe-deposit boxes because there'd be fewer of them, but you'd follow the same procedures if you had to check accounts. With the boxes you'd be looking for ones that were rented after the first of April—Riggott didn't buy the Atlantic stock until the second. It would be the same thing with checking or savings accounts."

"How would you go about it?"

"Well, beginning with boxes, you'd get a list of recent renters from each bank. Then you'd sit down with telephone and city directories going back several years and check off names. You'd eliminate most of the list right there. People who had been established at the same address and in the same occupation for years would be out of the picture. There wouldn't be too many left."

"Even so—wouldn't it be easier to check first for accounts or boxes under real names in other communities?"

"There must be at least two hundred banks in Connecticut," Jim pointed out. "The state banking commissioner can give you the exact figures if you want them. And it's not a mere matter of walking in and asking for a list of their depositors and the rest of the information you'd want. No indeed. Banks guard their records like the gold at Fort Knox. I'd be untangling red tape for years."

They were talking quietly, but now that it was nearly dark Jim was conscious of the ease with which anyone could approach the cottage and listen to their conversation. He changed the subject by asking, "What do you think it will run to if we have to buy Elaine a new dress?"

"It's silk shantung and it's well made. I would have said thirty-five or forty dollars, but when she told me she bought it at Lansing's I upped the figure another ten or so. They're about the best dress shop in Hampton."

"Uh-huh." It was too dark for Margaret to see the meditative expression that settled on her husband's face, but his tone reflected it. "Isn't that quite a lot for her to pay for a dress on Dean's income?" he inquired. "Do you pay that much for yours?"

"Not very often; never for summer dresses. But then I have my own system of buying. I watch for end of the season sales at the good shops and buy when they've marked their things away down."

Jim was amused by the note of conscious virtue in her voice, but he offered her the tribute she expected. "Nice thrifty wife I've got . . . You don't pay that kind of money for dresses and yet I probably earn close to

162

three times as much as Dean does."

"Yes, I know. I don't have a charm bracelet either. He bought her one."

"They cost a lot?"

"I should think there's over two hundred dollars tied up in hers. He bought a new charm for it at Easter and it must have cost at least fifty dollars. She wouldn't have anything inexpensive. All her things run into more money than you'd expect."

Jim said, "Uh-huh," again. Then, "It looks as if he made a nice piece of change on the stock market."

"He must have. She was driving her own car today."

"Her own car? I took it for granted she came in Dean's."

"I haven't had a chance to tell you about it. She had her own car."

"Do you mean a new one?"

"No, it's a '50 Chevy convertible. It's in beautiful condition, though. Looks like new." Margaret's tone carried a trace of uncertainty. She didn't know where the conversation was taking them. She went on, "Elaine said Dean got a real buy on it at Grimaldi's. Only six hundred and fifty. But from what she said, he didn't pay cash for it, he's buying it on time."

"Six hundred and fifty?" Jim spoke incredulously. "He must have paid more than that. If it's in such good condition."

"That's what she told me he paid. At Grimaldi's."

Jim made no further comment. Margaret waited for it, but he was silent looking out over the lake.

She stood up and walked to the screen door and couldn't quite keep a nervous tremor out of her voice as she said, "Even six-fifty is a lot for people in their position. And there's the running expenses of two cars."

"Yes, you're right." Jim got to his feet and said with sudden briskness, "I guess I'll see if I can catch me a fish."

Thirteen

When the county detective reached Hampton the next morning he drove straight to Grimaldi's, entering the enormous used-car lot under a sign that announced flamboyantly that Grimaldi, aiming to please his customers, sold the best used cars in town at the lowest prices.

Jim was directed to the office in the center of the lot, where he found Grimaldi talking down a man who seemed, from the conversation, to be a less-than-pleased customer. The car-lot owner was small and slight with white hair that stood up in a crest in front, flashing dark eyes, and a loud, rapid voice. He gesticulated, he clasped his head, he proclaimed his record for square dealing with an eloquence that overwhelmed the customer and finally reduced him to silence. The last Jim saw of him he was being ushered to the door, his expression dazed, and was there turned over to one of a swarm of salesmen.

Grimaldi threw his smile into high gear and advanced on Jim. "What can I do for you, sir?" he asked.

His smile vanished, his eyes went wary when Jim identified himself. "What's the trouble?" he asked.

"There's no trouble," the county detective replied. "I'm just looking for some information about a car you sold for six hundred and fifty dollars—a '50 Chevy convertible in first-class condition."

Grimaldi's hand went to his head. "Six-fifty—in first-class condition? Mr. O'Neill, our prices are the lowest you'll find anywhere—anywhere at all"—his sweeping gesture took in the universe—"and the best buys for the money. But"—his loud voice dropped dramatically—"we don't give cars away. We're not in business for our health."

Jim, bearing with these antics, nodded. "I thought the price was too low. Now, about the sale—" He proceeded to give the car-lot owner the data he had on Elaine's car. The latter rushed to his bookkeeper eager to co-operate and prove what a clear conscience he had. The bookkeeper produced the invoice of the sale of the convertible to Dean a week earlier. The price was one thousand dollars plus thirty-seven for the sales tax and the car registration. The invoice was marked paid in full.

"There, you see?" Grimaldi exclaimed triumphantly. "A fair price, yes. A gift, no. People," he continued, throwing wide his hands, "the way their minds work. I suppose this fellow is bragging to his friends about what a buy he got, huh?"

"That's the way it goes," Jim answered.

Grimaldi pursed his lips and threw the detective a glance of liveliest curiosity. "But no, there must be more than that to the story. Otherwise you wouldn't be here."

Jim smiled at him pleasantly and turned to the bookkeeper. "How was the car paid for? Cash or a check?"

The bookkeeper consulted the invoice. "By check. The key number on it is 51-907 over 111."

Jim wrote down the number. "You don't know what bank that is, I suppose."

"No, I'm afraid I don't. You'll have to get that from the state banking commissioner."

Jim thanked the bookkeeper and Grimaldi and had some difficulty in shedding the latter, who followed him out to his car assuring him of his readiness to be of help at any and all times.

Jim went to his office and phoned the office of the bank commissioner. He was told that the key number on Dean's check indicated it had been drawn on the Woodville Savings Bank.

After he had replaced the receiver he sat back for an interval in thought. Woodville was in Hampton County about thirty miles from the city itself. It was a manufacturing town with a population of ten or twelve thousand and Jim could think of no ties Dean would have with it.

Up to this point the county detective had been neutral in his attitude toward the young man. He had followed up the price of the car not only because it seemed too low but because of Margaret's comments on the cost of Elaine's bracelet and all her things. It looked as if Elaine, apparently telling what she thought was the truth about what the car had cost and that it was being bought on time, didn't know how much money her husband had. Although he indulged her expensive tastes in many ways he must have lied to her about the car to conceal the extent of his prosperity.

Jim decided he'd better go to Woodville and see what Dean's checking account showed.

He took care of his mail and a few other matters first. Then he set out for Woodville.

The twelve o'clock factory whistles were blowing as he entered the town. By the time he found a place to park near the bank and went in, everyone with enough authority to deal with his inquiries had left for lunch. It was the kind of minor delay to which he had long since become accustomed. He hunted up a restaurant and had lunch himself.

When he returned to the bank he was referred to its secretary, who made a profound study of the authorization from Goodrich that Jim had been using all through the investigation. The county detective was accustomed to that, too, having spent much of his time in banks since the night Leonard's body was found. He lit a cigarette and waited. Presently the ledger card covering Dean's account would be produced.

When it was laid before him it disclosed that the account had been opened on April 20 with a cash deposit of seventeen hundred dollars. The checks that had been drawn against it were for sums no larger than one hundred dollars with the exception of one check for $1037 that had been charged to the account the day before. Elaine's car, Jim thought, and it left in the account only $53.35. The windfall made on the market, if that was what it was, was almost used up.

He asked about a safe-deposit box and learned Dean hadn't rented one there. Then he asked if he could talk with the teller who had opened the account. The latter was summoned and remembered opening it.

"We don't get many accounts from out-of-town people unless they work in Woodville," he explained. "But Mr. Lipscomb did say he and his wife were looking around in this section for a place to live."

"You didn't ask him if he had an account in any other bank or for local references?" Jim inquired.

"No, I didn't. He was opening the account with cash, you see."

That was all the information the bank could give the county detective. But it was enough to furnish him with food for thought on the drive back to Hampton.

Dean Lipscomb, with seventeen hundred in cash, had deposited it in an out-of-town bank where it might well have escaped scrutiny forever. An extravagant, demanding wife could have been his sole reason for doing it, but Jim had to ask himself if there was an additional one: Was Dean concealing assets not only from Elaine but from the police? And did he have other assets hidden in other banks?

The field was wide, Jim recognized. Dean came from Philadelphia; he might have an account or a safe-deposit box there. Or he might have either one in Connecticut under his own or an assumed name.

Before he arrived back in Hampton the county detective, reviewing his whole acquaintance with Dean, recalled that Tad had made some reference two or three months ago to Dean's having turned in an older car for the '51 model he had been driving since Jim had known him.

As soon as he reached his office Jim called the Motor Vehicle Department and learned that the license plates on Dean's former car, a 1946 Plymouth, had been transferred to his 1951 Plymouth on April 22, and that he had bought the newer car at Grimaldi's.

This time, Jim thought, he could put his questions to the car-lot owner over the phone.

Grimaldi was as eager as ever to assist the county detective. He asked him to hold the line while he referred to his records and came back on it a few minutes later with the information that Dean, in addition to turning in his old car, had paid seven hundred and fifty in cash for the newer model he had bought.

That gave Jim another substantial sum of money in Dean's possession to think about. The date of the sale was also of interest; April 22 was only two days before the date of Riggott's murder.

It was beginning to add up to something. He had better lay it before Goodrich.

When he had heard the story the state's attorney thought that their first move should be to find out if Dean actually had made money on the stock market. "How about asking Beecher if he knows anything about it?" he said.

"According to what Elaine Lipscomb told my wife, Beecher doesn't know the first thing about it. I can feel him out on it, though."

"You'd better do that. Then there are all the other brokerage firms."

"Yes," Jim said, and then, "My God, what a case. Banks and brokers."

Goodrich chuckled. "At least they all know you now. They'll treat you like a blood brother when you make the rounds this time."

"They'd better hold my hand," Jim replied. "I need it."

Goodrich was toying with his glasses, which hung suspended on a black ribbon. He swung them to and fro as he said, "Theft of the bonds wouldn't prove murder. For that matter, with Riggott dead, how do we prove the bonds were stolen? The young man could say Riggott made him a gift of them. We'd know he didn't, but if Lipscomb stuck to it that he did, he could give us a hell of a time. If he kept the Atlantic certificate, it would be a different story, of course. With Riggott's name on it, he could hardly say Riggott gave it to him. He'd be very foolish, though, if he kept it."

"If he didn't intend to keep it, why take it?" Jim inquired. "I think it was in the safe with the bonds and when they were taken, the certificate was taken. If Lipscomb did it, he must have had it in mind that he'd hang on to it for a while and then try to unload it. Look at its face value; over seven thousand. It would go against human nature to destroy it."

"That's true. But if he didn't have some second thoughts regarding it after the murder came to light, then he's the worst kind of fool. It would mean a lot to us, naturally, if he did keep it."

Jim made no reply. They were getting ahead of themselves, he felt. They had nothing yet on Dean and here was the state's attorney looking ahead to the kind of evidence he could bring into a courtroom against the young man. Jim preferred to work one step at a time.

Goodrich said next, "This thing seems promising, but if it's a false alarm we've simply got to do something about Saxton. He's been my choice all along. The case is over a month old and we'll have to bear down on him if the Lipscomb angle doesn't take us anywhere."

"We've tried it already," Jim answered. "It did no

good. We can't even show that he might have been in such desperate straits for money that he stole from his uncle."

"The safe wasn't tampered with. He's the one most likely to have known the combination."

"Well, if he knew it, he also knew his uncle would realize right away he was the thief and would cut him off from an inheritance that's going to run close to a quarter of a million."

"You're taking too rigid a view of this, Jim. You're convinced the theft preceded and brought on the murder. It doesn't have to be that way. Saxton could have killed his uncle for other reasons and taken the bonds after he was dead. He had a key to the apartment; he could have taken them at any time. Maybe, if he was in desperate need of money at the time of the murder, he cashed the bonds and used the proceeds to straighten out his affairs so that they look good now."

"You're leaving out the Atlantic certificate," Jim reminded him. "Why take that? He couldn't be sure of disposing of it at anything near its face value, but if he left it in the safe he'd inherit half of it when the estate was settled."

"Oh, for heaven's sake," Goodrich exclaimed, with a trace of irritation. "We never tie up all the loose ends in a murder. Maybe he took it by mistake and didn't have the nerve to put it back. Or the opportunity."

This was the feeblest kind of reasoning, Jim thought. But Goodrich was the state's attorney; if he didn't recognize it for what it was, it wasn't the county detective's place to point it out to him.

They had worked together many years. When Jim

remained silent the state's attorney had no trouble following his thoughts. He said, "All right, Saxton had plenty of opportunity to put it back if he took it by mistake. But at least with him we have the possibility that he knew the combination of the safe, whereas with Lipscomb there's no way he would have known it. You don't think Riggott gave it to him, do you?"

"No, I don't."

"Then how do you think he got hold of those bonds?"

"I haven't any idea. But"—Jim got to his feet—"maybe I'd better start trying to find out. I'll give Tad Beecher a ring and ask him to have a drink with me. It's four o'clock and he usually knocks off for the day around this time."

Tad was still in his office. He said sure, he'd be glad to meet Jim for a drink before going to the lake. His tone expressed surprise. "I thought you were so deep in murder these days you had no time for being social."

"Well, I'm through early today. Shall I meet you at Simon's?" This was a small bar midway between their offices.

"Fine," Tad agreed. "See you there in about fifteen minutes."

They were on their second drink before Jim brought up Dean's name. Then he began, "Margaret told me Elaine drove out to our place yesterday in her own car. Dean bought it for her last week, she said."

Tad's round face revealed astonishment. "You sure about that? Dean hasn't mentioned it to me."

"Oh yes, I'm sure. Elaine said he bought it at Grimaldi's and got an excellent buy on it."

"Well, I'll be damned." Tad stared into his glass with

a thoughtful frown. "Kid's crazy," he stated a moment later. "He can't afford two cars. I'm only paying him seventy-five a week, Jim. He'll be earning more pretty soon, but he's got no business living on his expectations." He shook his head. "He's probably up to his neck in debt on account of that wife of his. You know how he feels about her. Whatever she wants he's going to bust a gut to get it for her. She's got him just where she wants him."

"It looks that way," Jim said.

"I guess he'd rather not tell me about it," Tad resumed, after taking a swallow from his glass. "He knows my views on young people getting in debt." His frown deepened as personal feelings came to the fore. "Chrissake, I'm trying to give the kid a start, I've tried to be nice to both of them and Phoebe, she ran her legs off looking for an apartment for them that would be within their means. So what happens? He goes into debt to buy Elaine a car. And he doesn't even mention it to me."

"Maybe he didn't go into debt for it," Jim suggested. "Maybe he was able to pay cash for it."

"Not a chance! He hasn't got a dime beyond his salary and I know his father is in no position to hand him money for cars. Where else would he get it?"

Jim slid his glass back and forth on the table and studied the wet track it made. "Perhaps he picked up a few hundred on the market."

"I should say not. I won't have that sort of thing going on at my place. We're investment brokers, not speculators."

"Well, some other broker—"

"Not in Hampton, no sir. He'd know it would get

back to me."

"There's New York. There's Philadelphia."

"No, he—" Tad broke off. He glanced in doubt at Jim. "He did say something once about Webster and Hayes in Philadelphia. They're a big investment house and he had some sort of contact with them at one time or another."

Tad, who had no notion of what was in Jim's mind, went on to a dissertation on the spartan economy Phoebe and he had had to practice in the first years of their marriage; on how his father, at that time the head of Beecher's, had preached the gospel of thrift to him and all the employees of the firm.

Tad held strong views on the subject, Jim realized. There was no doubt about it, if Dean had been playing the market, he needed to conceal it from Tad; while from Elaine he needed to conceal how much money he'd made to prevent her spending it overnight. He'd have a double-barreled motive, therefore, in secreting stock-market winnings in an out-of-town bank.

This was a disheartening thought. It brought Jim back to the blank wall he'd faced yesterday.

He said no more about Dean. Tad and he finished their second drink and started, one car in back of the other, for the lake.

When Jim arrived home he found Margaret and the children in a circle looking at something on the grass, Margaret holding Rex back as he barked at the top of his lungs and struggled to break free of her grip on his collar. Off to one side Juney sat regarding the group with sleepy-eyed detachment.

Rex was making so much noise that Jim's arrival went unnoticed.

"What goes on here?" he called, as he walked toward them.

Margaret turned and tightened her grip on Rex who made wilder efforts to free himself when he saw Jim.

"Oh Jim, it's a baby rabbit. It's dead."

"Juney killed it," mourned Loria with tears in her eyes. "He killed it dead and brought it in the yard."

"He's a bad, bad cat!" Sarah shook her finger at Juney. "Bad, bad boy."

Juney twitched a whisker.

Jim took over control of Rex, cuffing him lightly and saying, "Shut up, you. You're jealous," and bending over the limp bundle of tan fur on the grass. "Now it's rabbits," he commented. "What a hunter that cat is."

"I could do with less of it," Margaret declared. "I'm tired of finding dead mice and rats and birds on the doorstep. To say nothing of finding half ones."

"If he doesn't bring home his kill, how are we to know he's a mighty hunter?" asked Jim.

"Poor little rabbit." Loria's tears spilled over on her cheeks.

"You can have a funeral for it," Margaret said, patting her shoulder. "There's a box in the broom closet you can use. You get it, darling, and we'll put the rabbit in it. Then you and Sarah can pick flowers to put on the grave."

"Can I dig the grave, Mommy?" Sarah asked.

"I want to dig it," Loria said.

"You can take turns digging it," Jim put in.

"Well, while you're getting it done I'll go ahead with dinner," Margaret announced, and started for the cottage dragging a protesting Rex with her and calling back over her shoulder, "You'll have to bury it good and deep if you don't want Rex to dig it up."

At the table that night Sarah developed a fractious mood. She wanted to go to a drive-in theater. Several times that summer Jim had refused her, saying she was too young and certainly Loria was too young to be kept out of bed for that sort of project. Now, for some obstinate eight-year-old reason, Sarah renewed her plea. "Daddy, can't we go to a drive-in tonight?"

"No."

"But it gets dark much earlier and the show starts earlier and we wouldn't be out very late."

"No." Jim, whose thoughts were on Dean Lipscomb, hadn't been emphatic in pronouncing his first no. But the second one had enough emphasis and a frown accompanied it.

Sarah was willfully blind to the frown and to her mother's warning glance. She said in self-pitying accents, "Gee, all the kids go but me. Every single one of them. I'm the only one that's never gone to a drive-in. I don't see why I can't go just once to see what they're like. It's so crazy to be the only one that's never—"

"Sarah, I don't want to hear another word. I said no and that's the end of it."

"Gee, Daddy—"

Margaret bit her lip in annoyance. Why wouldn't Sarah show some sense and shut up?

Sarah wouldn't. She became more aggressive. She couldn't ever do the things other kids did. All she ever heard was no, no, no . . .

Her father sent her from the table. She burst into tears sobbing defiantly, "All right, see if I care. If you want to be so mean when all the other kids—"

Jim got to his feet. "Go straight to bed, young lady. And if I hear one more word out of you, I'll give you a spanking you'll remember."

Sarah knew from experience that he meant it. She fled, her sobs rising to wails.

Loria had stopped eating to devote her attention to the scene between her father and sister. She picked up her spoon again, remarking smugly, "My, Sarah was naughty. I'm glad I'm not naughty like that."

Jim's eyes met Margaret's. He checked an impulse to laugh.

After dinner he went outdoors. His gaze turned automatically to the cottage next door. There it stood shuttered and drawn in upon itself. It knew who had killed its owner, but it had yielded nothing of its knowledge to all their tests and searchings.

Without purpose or expectation, Jim walked over to it. He still had a key to the back door. He unlocked it and went inside to climb the stairs to the room where he had found the body. In the faint light that came in through the shutters it had a look of complete abandonment although actually it was much the same as it had been in Leonard's lifetime. The only thing that had been removed from it was the bed clothing, which had been sent to the Identification Bureau.

There was nothing to hold the county detective there. He went back downstairs into the living room, which stretched across the front of the cottage. The shutters were closed; the air hot and stale. He opened the front door and one of the windows, raising the blind and throwing back the shutters. Now there was light and air let in on the staleness and gloom, but not on the problem of who was the murderer.

Jim sat down by the window and looked out at the lake. The cottage was very still. There was something in its stillness, though—his knowledge, perhaps, of how it had once been broken—that prevented him from settling down for an interval of quiet, concentrated thought.

After a few minutes he got up to leave; he would find no help, no inspiration here. As he leaned out to draw the shutters, the sun, low in the west, picked out on the window sill a design—$\Sigma\Pi$—that looked like a doodle someone had scratched there. Jim eyed it trying to think what there was about it that was familiar. He had no success. There were many scratches on the window sill. The familiar look of the two he studied was probably accidental, he decided. He drew the shutters, locked up the cottage, and went out on the lake to fish.

It was close to ten o'clock when he returned in triumph with three trout. He displayed them to his wife saying, "Look, three browns. We'll have them for breakfast."

The children had long been asleep. Margaret followed Jim outdoors and sat down on the back steps to keep him company while he cleaned the fish. The porch light coned out into darkness. No other cottage except the Saxtons' showed a light.

"The Beechers and Loretta must be out," Margaret remarked.

"Tad had tickets for the Show Shop. He and Phoebe were taking the Lipscombs."

"Loretta's new man was out here at last tonight," Margaret informed her husband. "He was sitting on the porch with her earlier. They must have gone somewhere."

"You hope." Jim gave her a broad grin. "Not a sign of a light over there."

"She could sue you for that. It's slander."

"You're no witness. Wife can't testify against her husband." Jim decapitated a trout with one stroke.

Margaret wasn't listening. Her thoughts had turned to the Lipscombs. She said, "I called Elaine today. She thinks the cleaner will be able to get the grape juice out of her dress."

"Good. Money in our pocket."

"Yes, but—" Margaret came to a halt. Then she went on, "Along with the dress and the new car there was another incident yesterday that I didn't tell you about and I've been thinking perhaps I should. It was the way she acted over her ring."

Margaret described what Elaine's attitude had been, what she had said, and concluded, "So I've been wondering—"

"If it's another expensive present Dean bought her just recently?"

"I guess that's it." She gave him a doubtful glance. "I should mind my own business. You're the detecting end of the family."

"I'm not doing too well at it right now," Jim said.

"You'll work it out," she assured him. "Your problem is that there was too much time to get rid of the evidence."

"I doubt there ever was much. Except the gun. That's in the Connecticut River long ago."

"It is a handy way to get rid of it."

"Yes." Jim's tone was dry. "Every time I question a crook about one he says he threw it in the river."

"Don't you ever get them back?"

180

"My dear, we don't try. They sink in the mud." Jim finished cleaning the last fish and stood up wiping the scales from his knife on a newspaper. "So I'm not going to get this gun," he said.

"You'll find some other evidence."

"Sure I will. I have to. I've got four—no, six, counting Juney and Rex—mouths to feed."

Margaret smiled up at him. "Do you mind too much?"

He bent and kissed her. "Couldn't get along without them."

"That's what I wanted you to say," she stated contentedly.

Fourteen

Jim couldn't take Tad's word for it that if Dean had been buying stock through any other broker in Hampton, news of it would get back to Beecher's. He had to verify this for himself and it took the greater part of three days visiting every broker in the city itself and the suburbs to do it.

The first day he sent an inquiry through state police headquarters to the Philadelphia police asking if their records showed a gun registered in Dean's name; and also if they would find out from Webster and Hayes if Dean had carried an account with that firm during the past year.

At the end of the second day Cobb and Bailo, who had been making the rounds of the brokers while Jim was busy on another case, reported that with seven remaining to be seen, the results were completely negative. Jim said they could call on the last seven the next morning. He would phone the New York and Boston firms that had direct lines to Hampton.

His telephone rang. The state police communications officer was on the line. He informed Jim that the Philadelphia police had reported back that they had no record of Dean ever registering for a gun; and that the young man had made one stock purchase in the amount of twenty dollars through Webster and Hayes five years ago and none since.

When Jim hung up and told Cobb and Bailo what he had just learned Cobb said, "So now we're branching out. We're going to check every broker in the country."

The county detective grinned at him. "It's not going to be that bad. I'll settle for the ones around here; and it begins to look as if he didn't have an account with any of them."

"Nice if he'd had a permit for an Iver-Johnson on file in Philadelphia," Bailo remarked.

"You like things made too easy," Cobb reproved him.

"Sure I do," Bailo agreed. He said to Jim, "If Lipscomb's got those bonds, where d'you suppose he stashed them away?"

"Safe deposit," Jim replied.

Cobb groaned.

On the way to the lake that night the county detective considered what his next step should be. Checking safe-deposit lists for an assumed name would be a prolonged business, its outcome uncertain. If Dean had the bonds—and the if was getting smaller in Jim's mind—there ought to be some way of working out a short cut to locate them.

Before noon the next day Cobb and Bailo reported that they had visited the last seven brokerage houses in Hampton and that Dean had not done business with any of them.

Jim took this information to Goodrich. Then he laid before the latter the plan he had evolved last night for testing whether or not Dean had the bonds and, if he did have them, getting him to reveal their place of concealment.

Goodrich thought the plan had merit. He added, "The thing is, I wish you didn't have to enlist Beecher's aid to work it out."

"I'll tell him as little as possible," Jim said.

"Well, its worth a try." The state's attorney's tone was still dubious. "We'll just have to hope he'll keep his mouth shut."

It was Friday. Banks and investment houses would be closed over the week end. Jim waited, therefore, until Sunday evening to talk with Tad. The latter was sitting alone on the dock in front of his cottage when Jim dropped down beside him and said, "There's something I need your help on—if you don't mind giving it and at the same time keeping it under your hat."

"Why—sure." Tad's tone reflected the seriousness of Jim's. "What's it all about?"

"Dean Lipscomb. I'd like you to tell him you just heard such and such a stock is going to be split two for one or that there's going to be a merger with another company that will triple its value or whatever you think would make the best story. I'll leave that part to you. Tell him you know he could use some extra money and that this is his chance to make it if he can lay his hands on a couple of thousand right away quick."

"But"—Tad gaped at him—"I don't know of any deal like that coming up right now. And Dean hasn't got that kind of money."

"He might be able to get it."

"I can't imagine where—but if he did and brought it to me—where would I be then?"

"You'd just accept the money. I'd take over from that point on."

"But Dean knows the market. I don't think he'd go along with a story like that."

"He will if you give it to him as an inside tip. When you've figured out what you're going to tell him you can say news of the merger or split or whatever it is won't become public for another month or two, that it's still a deep dark secret and you're letting him in on the ground floor."

"Well . . ." Tad fell silent for a space. He looked worried and unhappy. At last he said, "Just tell me one thing, Jim. Has this got something to do with Len's murder?"

"Yes—if it comes to anything."

"But I—"

"Please," Jim interrupted him. "I'm sorry, but I can't go into detail with you. We don't work that way. I'd just like to have you tell Dean what I suggested. If he asks for time off to try to get the money, tell him he can have it. Whatever he wants to do, go along with it, will you? Then let me know what he says."

Again Tad fell silent studying an unlighted cigar he held in his hand. "I don't like it," he declared presently. "Not a bit. But I suppose"—he bent an anxious gaze on Jim—"it's my duty as a citizen to do it."

"I would say so." Jim, respecting his scruples, gave him a reassuring smile. "Don't you realize the police couldn't get by without help from private citizens?"

"But with Dean it's a little different. I brought him

185

here and—".

"I know how you feel. It's too bad. Will you call me tomorrow as soon as you've talked to him?" Jim's tone was firm, putting an end to Tad's protests. "To be on the safe side you'd better use an outside phone."

Tad called the county detective at ten the next morning. "I'm at the drugstore down the street," he said. "I told him the story I fixed up. He fell right in with it. He was so pleased. He thinks he knows where he can raise a couple of thousand. From an uncle, he said. When he asked how soon he ought to have the money I told him the sooner the better. That was what you wanted, wasn't it?"

"Yes, that's it. You handled it very well."

"Then he wanted to know if it would be all right if he didn't come in tomorrow. His uncle lives in Providence, he said, and he'd like to give him a call and arrange to see him. I told him to go right ahead."

"Good. It's really working out."

"I'm glad you think so." Tad spoke without satisfaction. "Look, Jim, if he does have an uncle he can borrow from and shows up the day after tomorrow with the two thousand I'm going to be in a hell of a spot."

"Don't worry about it. I'll take over when he gets the money." Jim's tone was confident. Dean had risen to the bait.

Dean himself exuded confidence Tuesday morning setting off for New York. Tad was sharing an inside tip with him, giving him the chance to triple his money in a matter of months. Tad had said he didn't do that sort of thing as a rule; that he was doing it just this once because he knew the merger was a sure thing and he wanted to see Dean get some money ahead. His manner had been stiff and abrupt while he was making the offer to Dean. He didn't approve of what he was doing, the latter thought, but he was going ahead with it regardless. That showed how much interest he took in Dean.

Edging his car in and out of the early morning traffic Dean smiled as he recalled the older man's manner. Tad was a good egg. He'd been kindness itself from the day Dean arrived in Hampton.

"Too bad I can't come back with three thousand," Dean reflected. "He did say a couple of thousand, but wouldn't he think it was all right if I told him Uncle Ike was willing to loan me three? I don't see why not. Then, if I triple the money, I'd have nine thousand instead of six. Nice going. No wonder they say money breeds money."

Cobb and Bailo were following him in separate cars. He didn't notice them. There was no reason he should. Over a month had gone by since the murder was discovered and there hadn't been a sign of suspicion pointing toward him. He felt perfectly safe from it.

He was five minutes early for his train. While Cobb kept an eye on him Bailo telephoned Jim, who was already at his office, to tell him Dean had bought a ticket for the eight forty-five train to New York.

"Both of you stay with him," Jim said. "I'll put in a call to New York. Let's see, who do I know at Centre Street?"

"Captain Lucas on the main office squad," Bailo suggested.

187

"Yes, he's the one I want. I'll ask him to hav[e] someone at the station to meet you."

Jim broke the connection. So New York was Dean'[s] destination he was thinking as he pressed the interco[m] button on his phone to buzz Jenny. Did he have a safe deposit box there?

He had Jenny put through a person-to-person call t[o] Captain Lucas.

He was still at his office waiting to hear what ha[d] happened when Cobb arrived at five-thirty tha[t] afternoon. As soon as he appeared his pleased expression told Jim the trip had been a success.

"He's got the bonds," the big detective announced. "In safe deposit at the Madison Avenue Trust Company. He cashed three of them right there in the bond department where he knows one of the sales-men."

"Well," said Jim with deep satisfaction.

Cobb sat down and told him about the trip. Dean had read all the way to New York, he hadn't even looked around to see who was in the same coach with him. At Grand Central a detective from Centre Street, armed with their descriptions, was waiting for them. Dean had made their task easy by walking from the railroad station to the bank, not once glancing behind him or taking the smallest precaution against the possibility of being followed. It was apparent that he had no thought of such a thing.

At the bank while Dean went to the safe-deposit vault the detective from Centre Street talked to one of the officials; no difficulties were made about giving them the information that Dean was renting the box ınder his own name. He sold the bonds right there in he bank.

After he left, with Bailo trailing him, Cobb and the Centre Street detective talked with the salesman in the bond department who had bought the bonds from Dean. It was the second time he had handled such a transaction, he said. His records showed that the first time had been on April 15; on that date Dean had sold four of the bonds.

The young fellow in the bond department was pretty upset over the whole thing, Cobb said. They hadn't told him what was behind their inquiries, but he knew something was wrong and he was the one who had vouched for Dean.

When they finished their business at the bank Cobb and the Centre Street detective separated and Cobb went back to the railroad station. He had his lunch there and waited for Dean and Bailo to appear. They arrived in time for the three of them to catch the two-ten train back to Hampton. Dean had headed toward home, Bailo following him, while Cobb had come back to the office to make his report.

"What did he do after he left the bank?" Jim asked.

"Had a drink and ate lunch at a place off Madison, Bailo said, and when he came out of there he just walked around looking in windows killing time until the two-ten and acting like he didn't have a care in the world." Cobb added, "So that's that. And what's the next move?"

"I think that's all for you fellows for tonight. I'll call Hildreth and ask him to have someone from his department take over from Bailo. In the morning Bailo can tail Lipscomb to Beecher's. You report in here. Goodrich has gone home. After I've called Hildreth I'll give him a ring and let him figure out what we do next."

"We're going to need more than those bonds for evidence," Cobb stated. "Unless he confesses."

"He probably won't," Jim observed, reaching for the telephone. "Life isn't that simple."

Fifteen

Dean turned over three thousand dollars to Tad the next morning. "I know you mentioned two," he said, making his tone and smile diffident. "But when I told Uncle Ike about the wonderful break you were giving me he insisted on loaning me three thousand. He said he could spare it all right and there was no hurry about returning it. I hope you don't mind or have the feeling that I'm overreaching myself."

"Not at all. Glad you could get the extra thousand." Tad accepted the thick roll of bills Dean held out to him. "I'll write you a receipt for this."

He spoke in a slow, constrained voice. He couldn't bring himself to look at Dean as he drew a pad toward him, wrote down the date, and "Received from Dean Lipscomb the sum of three thousand dollars for investment." He signed his name, tore the sheet from the pad, and handed it to the young man.

The latter, putting it in his wallet, said, "I can't tell you how much I appreciate your doing this. It's going to be a tremendous help to Elaine and me."

"It's quite all right." Tad forced himself to smile and raise his eyes to Dean's face. It was, however, such a stiff little smile that Dean thought, "He's embarrassed to death over the whole thing; he doesn't want to talk about it."

Tad's telephone rang just then. As he reached for the receiver, Dean said, "Thanks a lot," sketched a gay little salute, and moved away. His step was light. He felt as if he were walking on air.

Jim was on the phone. He inquired, "Okay to ask a question?"

"Yes." Through the open door of his office Tad's gaze rested on Dean who had stopped at the board and was looking at the quotations the board boy chalked up.

"Did he bring it in?"

"Yes."

"Three thousand instead of two?"

"Yes." Tad was too confused by the way the situation was developing to wonder how Jim knew a larger amount of money was involved.

"I see. Thank you, Tad. I'll talk to you later."

Jim was in Goodrich's office. He hung up and said to the state's attorney, "He's given Beecher the money."

Goodrich stared past him out the window. "I guess we'd better bring him in now for questioning. I wish we had more on him, though. But it's hard to see where or how we're going to get it. We'll have to try for a confession."

Jim made no reply. It was he who had settled on Dean as a suspect and done his best to gather evidence against him. He didn't expect Goodrich to say so; there was no reason he should. They had their separate

192

functions. Jim's was to gather the evidence, Goodrich's was to prosecute on it.

The county detective sent Cobb to bring in Dean. Bailo was already on the scene across the street from Beecher's, lounging against a building reading a newspaper. When he saw Cobb get out of his car he crossed over to join him.

"You wait out here in case he makes a break for it," Cobb said, and went inside.

Dean was at his desk. When Cobb halted in front of it he looked up at him and said inquiringly, "Yes?"

The big detective produced his badge. His heavy face was expressionless as he announced, "I'm from the state's attorney's office, Mr. Lipscomb. He wants me to bring you in for questioning in the Riggott murder."

Dean's face went gray, his eyes glassy from shock. He neither moved nor spoke. He was incapable of doing either. Other people weren't. Someone was talking on a telephone, one of the salesmen crossed his range of vision. Nobody seemed to realize that a pit had opened suddenly before him.

"The state's attorney wants to talk to you right away," Cobb prodded.

"Yes." Dean found a fragment of his voice. "Certainly."

It was an effort to get to his feet. His coat hung over the back of his chair. He put it on. He set one foot in front of the other and walked toward the door with Cobb close beside him. He stopped at Tad's office. "Mr. Beecher—" In his own ears his voice sounded far away.

Tad looked up, saw Dean's deathly color, saw Cobb who had police written all over him. Tad's face froze.

193

"Yes?" he said.

"I've got to go out awhile—" Dean cleared his throat trying to give his voice a more normal sound. "Something's come up—"

"All right," the older man said hurriedly. His glance avoided Dean's. He was the image of guilt.

They went outside. Cobb's car was parked a few feet from the door of Beecher's. Bailo fell in on the other side of Dean and Cobb said, "This is Detective Bailo."

In the car Dean sat between the two men. The first numbed moments were past. His mind began to work, dazedly, disconnectedly, but nevertheless to work, after a fashion, on his situation.

He was in a car with two detectives. They were taking him to the state's attorney to be questioned regarding Leonard Riggott's murder. The perfect murder, the murder that could never be laid at his door. . . .

The two detectives were as silent as he, Cobb maneuvering the car through traffic, Bailo, out of the tail of his eye, watching Dean.

He should have made some protest, demanded an explanation of what was in back of this, Dean thought. Letting himself be led away mute and stunned was a large point against him. An innocent man would have had plenty to say. What did the detective who had been sent for him think of his behavior? He glanced at Cobb's wooden profile. The latter would report Dean had come like a lamb, that his behavior indicated guilt.

Guilt had been shown by Tad too. He hadn't asked a single question; he hadn't needed to because he already knew what was going on. . . .

Dean's eyes followed unseeingly a woman who

crossed in front of the car when Cobb stopped for a red light. He was thinking about Tad. The latter had known what was going on, through having played some part in it.

The only part he could have played must be connected with the money Dean had got in New York yesterday.

Dean's heart dropped like a stone. That was it. They'd baited a trap for him and he'd walked right into it. He'd been followed to New York—they knew he had the bonds—oh God—

His thoughts began to race around and around the cage of his mind. What was he going to say? Oh God, what was he going to say?

He was turned over to Jim in the main office. The county detective said with distant courtesy, "Hello, Dean. We'll talk in Mr. Goodrich's office. You may be here awhile so if you'll give Mr. Cobb your keys, he'll get your car and drive it over here for you."

Dean hesitated. Why his car keys? He started to refuse the offer and thought better of it. If they wanted to look over his car, they'd do it with or without his consent. There was nothing incriminating in it anyway and, in the co-operative role he'd decided to play, he'd do well to go along with their suggestions.

He handed over the keys to Cobb and watched the detective go out through the door that opened on the corridor. On freedom. He had only to take the same route—no, of course he couldn't make a dash for it. He had to face this out.

He walked with Jim into Goodrich's office.

Jim performed the introduction. Goodrich stood up to acknowledge it, but he didn't offer his hand. Dean took the chair facing his desk and Jim dropped down in one near it.

The young man took the offensive he should have taken at Beecher's. "I don't understand what this is all about," he began, directing his words to Jim. "I told you what little I could about Mr. Riggott at the time his body was found. However—" He made a gesture that indicated he was, in the interests of law and order, at their disposal.

Goodrich, precise to the point of pedantry, said, "I believe you overlooked one or two matters, Mr. Lipscomb." He came to a full halt and left Dean in suspense while he removed his glasses, polished and replaced them. It was a favorite courtroom technique of his. When he had drawn it out to its fullest length he continued, "There were some bonds missing from Mr. Riggott's estate. Government threes, thirty-two of them, each one worth a thousand dollars. Mr. O'Neill says he did not mention them to you nor did you mention them to him. . . ."

So he was right, Dean thought. Tad's offer had been a trap. His glance went from one inscrutable face to the other. His heart pounded. It wouldn't do. He must pull himself together and meet his danger boldly.

He smiled in a way that was meant to be sheepish and uncertain although God only knew how it appeared to the two intent pairs of eyes that watched him. He said, "I hoped that point would never come up, Mr. Goodrich. I kept it back when Mr. O'Neill questioned me earlier in the summer. I have those bonds. They're in safe deposit in the Madison Avenue Trust Company in New York. I rented a box there last April a few days after Mr. Riggott gave them to me."

Jim realized instantly that Dean had figured out what they had on him. Had Tad given the show away? No, once he did what was asked of him there'd have been no sense in that. Dean himself had connected it with Tad's offer and now he had his answers ready. This was going to be tough. Tackling him so soon after his trip to New York meant they'd lost the advantage of surprise.

The county detective knew Goodrich's thoughts were following similar lines.

Both men were silent as Dean went on with his preposterous story whose preposterousness was going to be hard indeed to prove. "I rented a box in New York instead of here in Hampton because I didn't want to take the least chance of my wife finding out about Mr. Riggott's gift to me for a while. She'd have had a million plans for spending the money right away whereas I felt we should establish ourselves here in Hampton first—what with one thing and another we've been leading rather an unsettled life since our marriage—and then, when we'd bought a house and other things we needed, I'd let her know about Mr. Riggott's great kindness . . ."

Dean's voice flowed along without a break. "He gave me the bonds one night in April when I had dinner with him. The night I told you about, Mr. O'Neill." He looked at Jim and paused for acknowledgment.

"Yes." The county detective brought out the monosyllable in a flat voice grudging the acceptance it seemed to give to what the young man was saying.

"We went back to his apartment after we'd had dinner at his club and somehow I got talking about my problems, the slow start I was making and my wife's quite understandable impatience with it. Mr. Riggott kept encouraging me to talk until he had the whole picture. At about that time Mrs. Madler called, he went downstairs to see her, and I was left feeling that I'd said too much about my personal affairs. But when he came back I was utterly dumfounded by what he did. He went to his safe—it was in the den where we were sitting —opened it and took out a stack of bonds and handed it to me. He said things about having more money than he'd ever use and having known my father in college and that he'd taken a liking to me, and so on. He said he wanted to see Elaine and me make a go of our marriage and he was afraid it might break up over money troubles."

"He impressed it on me that I was to tell no one about it, that if it ever got back to his nephew it would cause hard feelings."

"I tried to say I couldn't accept a gift like that, but he wouldn't listen to me. He said put it away for now, try to work out my problems with Elaine without telling her I had it, and later on it would make things easier for us. . . ."

Goodrich's profile was turned toward Jim, but the latter could almost see waiting on his lips the question that would blow apart this fine-spun tale: "He also gave you a certificate that was made out in his name for forty shares of Atlantic stock?"

But Dean gave him no chance to ask it. He went on, "He put the bonds in a manila envelope. I was living in a furnished room at the time—my wife wasn't with me—and I didn't take them up to my room. I thought they'd be safer locked in my car. That's why I didn't find the stock certificate that was mixed in with them.

When I drove to New York a few days later and rented the box at the bank I still didn't find it. Aside from taking out four of the bonds, I left the envelope just as it was. I cashed the four I'd taken out there at the bank, planning that I could tell my wife I'd made a little money on the stock market. . . ."

"This was in April and yesterday was the first time I opened the box since the day I rented it. The stock certificate was in with the bonds I took out to cash and I was simply appalled when I came across it. I didn't know what to do; I couldn't think of a way to get it back to Mr. Riggott's estate without becoming involved in all kinds of explanations. I decided to leave it right where it was for the time being while I tried to figure out what to do about it."

Dean came to a halt. He waited for Goodrich and Jim to offer comment.

The state's attorney would take the lead. Jim sat back, reflecting that Dean had assembled his story plausibly and if he stayed with it they would have their troubles with him. His thoughts shifted to Cobb who was driving the young man's car to state police headquarters to turn it over to the Identification Bureau. The county detective hoped they would find some evidence in it that could be used against Dean.

The silence held. Dean found it disturbing. He couldn't control his sweat glands; he had to keep wiping trickles of sweat from his face and neck and hands. "That's about all I can tell you," he said.

Goodrich leaned forward, his elbows on his desk, his fingers steepled. His glance brooded over Dean as he said in his precise fashion. "That's quite a story, Mr. Lipscomb. It does credit to your imagination. Shall I pick out the grains of truth in it? There are a few. You seem to be intelligent enough to have mixed fact with fiction wherever possible."

"Look here, Mr. Goodrich—"

The state's attorney waved aside the protest. "You had dinner with Riggott at his club on the occasion you described. You did return to his apartment with him. He received a call from Mrs. Madler and left you alone while he went downstairs to talk with her. That was the night you got the bonds. That's all there is of truth in what you told us. The rest of it really went like this: You stole the bonds and the Atlantic certificate while Riggott was downstairs with Mrs. Madler. You—"

"I did nothing of the kind! He gave them to me." Dean threw indignation into his cry. He was settling down to what was, he recognized, a fight for his life. The method of murder he had used foretold a first-degree charge. A man who goes armed to an encounter with another cannot plead lack of premeditation.

"How could I have stolen them?" he demanded. "The bonds were in the safe. Do you think I blew it open and put it together again during the few minutes I was left alone in the apartment?"

There it was, Jim thought, one of the biggest holes in the case they could build against the young man. How had he got hold of the bonds? Any defense lawyer would have a field day with a question like that.

Goodrich was ready with an answer. But he wasn't in a court of law. He was at his desk and Dean had no lawyer to speak in his behalf. "You didn't steal the bonds from the safe," Goodrich declared. "Riggott had taken them out for some reason. That's how you came to get your hands on them."

The state's attorney was so wide of the mark that Dean felt encouraged. He asked, "Do you really think I'd be so foolish as to take them when I'd know that in a matter of hours—maybe only minutes—after I left Mr. Riggott would discover his loss?"

Jim was restive shifting around in his chair, his glance going back and forth between the two. The premature interview wasn't working out at all as Goodrich had intended it should. Dean showed no tendency to break down and confess to the murder.

"No," Goodrich replied, "but you didn't do it like that. You worked out some little angle on it that you thought would delay discovery of the theft or deflect suspicion from you."

"That isn't true. I won't stay here and listen to it!" Dean exclaimed.

"Yes you will." Goodrich fixed a cold eye on him and continued with his reconstruction of the case. Riggott, he said, finding out the bonds were missing, had known right away who had taken them. He had called Jim to ask if he would be at his office the next day. He hadn't gone to the police because of Dean's connection with Tad. He wanted the issue settled quietly.

"He talked to you about it and held Mr. O'Neill as a threat over your head," Goodrich said. "But you couldn't make full restitution even if you'd wanted to. You'd already cashed four of the bonds. You'd traded in your car for a newer one at Grimaldi's and paid the difference in cash. You'd bought gifts for your wife, a diamond ring, a gold charm for her bracelet."

Dean tried not to reveal his dismay over what they had been able to find out about his affairs. The resources they had for gathering information were

201

formidable. But there was a gap between information and proof, he encouraged himself.

Goodrich continued, "You saw him on Friday afternoon, April 23. He told you he would go to Mr. O'Neill the next day. That night you staged the vandalism at Mr. O'Neill's cottage to draw him away from his office Saturday morning at the time Riggott planned to see him. Then Riggott and you set out for the lake to talk to him there. On the way you pulled into the woods and shot Riggott. You hid his body in his cottage, counting on quite a bit of time going by before it was found . . ."

Goodrich's tone was inexorable. He hewed close to the actual facts as he covered every aspect of the murder, ignoring Dean's protests and denials. The latter took what comfort he could from the thought that as long as he insisted the bonds were a gift, the stock certificate mixed in with them by mistake, they couldn't prove he had a motive for killing Leonard Riggott.

Presently Jim took over. He began, "About the gun . . ."

Dean regarded questions about it as a breathing space. It was in the river along with Leonard's wallet and watch. They'd never trace its ownership to him. He said he'd never owned a gun, an Iver-Johnson or any other kind. Over and over he made this assertion.

At one o'clock he told them he was hungry. They had switched to a friendly approach at the moment. Goodrich was speaking in a fatherly manner, promising nothing in the way of leniency but seeming to promise much—if Dean would stop being stubborn and tell the truth about the murder.

The state's attorney sent out for sandwiches and coffee and the three of them ate there in his office. Then he questioning was resumed. When friendliness brought no results Goodrich adopted his cross-examining approach, one moment quick and biting, the next moment suave.

It was designed to bewilder the witness and it had that effect on Dean. The amount of effort he had to make in remaining constantly on his guard, weighing his every word, exhausted him. When Goodrich, talking about post-mortem lividity, slipped in the comment that Dean should have taken pains at the cottage to arrange the body in the exact position it had been in immediately after death, the young man almost defended himself, almost said, "I tried to do that. But I didn't notice the discoloration because I didn't want to look too closely at the face." He got as far as saying, "I—" and barely held back the rest of it.

"You what?" Goodrich pounced.

"I didn't kill him. I didn't have anything to do with how his body was arranged."

"That isn't what you started to say."

"Yes it is." Dean's handkerchief had become a limp rag. He mopped at his face with one of the paper napkins left over from their lunch and then looked at his watch. It was past four o'clock. He had been here for hours. He was worn down with questions. If he kept on answering them, he might make some such fatal break as he had just now nearly made. He set his jaw. He would stop answering them. He had some rights; they had no proof he was a murderer.

He said, "Mr. Goodrich, it's five minutes past four. I've been bearing with this patiently for nearly six hours. My reason for doing so is that I know how wrong I was in not telling Mr. O'Neill about the gift of the bonds as soon as the murder was discovered. Now I'm prepared to go all the way with you on them. I'll go to the bank in New York with someone from your office, take out the bonds and the stock certificate, and bring them back here for you to look at them. I cashed three of them yesterday and turned the money over to Mr. Beecher to invest it for me. There are still twenty-five bonds in my box."

Dean came to a stop, struck by misgivings. Maybe he shouldn't have made that offer. Maybe a lawyer would say he was sticking his neck out. But they knew he had them; they could probably get a court order to open the box. It seemed to him that the offer to produce them would be made by a man who actually was innocent of theft and murder and had nothing to fear from the police.

At intervals today he had thrown himself so wholeheartedly into his part that he had been on the verge of believing his own denials. It was an attitude he must build up in himself. It would give a ring of sincerity to everything he said.

When Goodrich didn't answer him right away but sat swinging his glasses on their ribbon and looking at him with a measuring eye Dean was emboldened to ask, "Does that meet with your approval? Or am I under arrest?"

"No," the state's attorney replied, "you're not under arrest. Not yet. You may go now—just a moment." He pressed the buzzer on his telephone and said to his secretary, "Have Mr. Lipscomb's car keys been left with you? . . . Thank you."

He hung up. "My secretary has your keys, Mr. Lipscomb. You may go home now. Detective Cobb will pick you up at your place at eight tomorrow morning and accompany you to New York. You're to turn the bonds and the stock certificate over to him and he will give you a receipt for them. Aside from the trip to New York I'll expect you to stay right here in Hampton and keep yourself available for further questioning."

Dean got to his feet. His legs felt like rubber. Now that the immediate threat was averted reaction was setting in. He said, "The way you talk, I think I'd better consult a lawyer."

"That is your privilege," Goodrich answered.

Dean picked up his keys in the outer office and was informed by Goodrich's secretary that his car was parked in back of the county court building. He followed the arrows along the corridor to the self-service elevator. When he stepped into it he had to lean against the wall for support. He was trembling all over.

He located his car in back of the building and collapsed in the seat. He no longer had to keep up a front or reassure himself with thoughts that there was no proof against him. He had committed a murder. They knew he had. They knew a lot about how he had carried it out and about all his other affairs too. Jim O'Neill must have been working like a beaver putting together the evidence they had.

Dean looked back fearfully at the great granite oblong of the court building. It stood for so much. Within its walls evidence was assembled, charges were made, trials were held, sentences pronounced. How many men had walked out of it to a death cell in the state prison?

When Dean felt composed enough to start home a new thought occurred to him. What should he say to Elaine? He would have to tell her something. Cobb would arrive in the morning to take him to New York there would be other complications, as yet unknown that couldn't be kept from her.

He sat where he was until he had reached a decision He would tell her the same story about the bonds tha he had told to the state's attorney and Jim. But he would minimize their suspicions of him.

As he drove away from the county court building he saw another car start up and follow his openly.

"God," he thought, "this can't be true. They can't be after me. I worked it all out so carefully—"

He drove fast. He wanted to get off the street and home to Elaine. If only she would be kind when he told her. She'd have to be kind at a time like this. He needed kindness from her with an urgent, aching need he'd never before experienced.

The other car was still in back of him when he turned into his street. He parked at the curb outside his door and rushed to its shelter, saying aloud, "Elaine . . ."

It didn't enter his mind that it was through buying her the car and other luxuries that he had led the police to him.

Sixteen

After dinner that night Jim took Sarah and Loria and Rex for a boat ride. He cut it as short as the protests of the children permitted, and as soon as he was back at the cottage he settled down to consider how Dean had opened the safe.

The county detective was convinced Riggott hadn't removed the bonds from it himself. If he had, Jim reasoned, Dean wouldn't have dared to steal them. It was only by taking them from the safe, which Riggott rarely opened, that Dean could hope their loss would go unnoticed for months, long enough to obscure the issue of who was responsible for it.

Jim referred to his notes on the safe. Its contents were listed as insurance policies, miscellaneous papers, the traveler's checks, and Leonard's passport. The passport, he remembered, had just been renewed.

Glenn had said his uncle had been more or less planning a trip to Italy. That accounted for the passport renewal. Then he decided to go to Vancouver instead. He wouldn't have needed his passport for that.

The county detective walked over to the Saxton cottage. He said to Glenn, "I'm interested in your uncle's passport. It had just been renewed around the time of his death. Did he have one particular travel agency that he generally booked with?"

"Yes, Watson's on Staunton Row."

"Thank you," said Jim.

When he returned home he found that Margaret, having put the children to bed, was preparing to go out for the evening with Phoebe Beecher. She kissed him good-by and left him to his brown study. She asked no questions. She knew that her husband, as he neared the end of a difficult case, didn't want to talk about it.

He went first to his office the next morning. There had been no reply yet to the request he had sent the Philadelphia police yesterday, asking for general information about Dean. It was too soon to expect one. He took care of his mail, discussed a morals case with Bailo, and soon after nine o'clock went to the travel agency.

The girl at the desk turned to her records. They showed that Leonard had brought in his passport on April 13 to have the agency take care of its renewal and that it had come back from the State Department and been picked up by him on April 23.

Jim returned to his office and phoned the manager of the Hampton Club, who looked in his files and then reported that April 12 two dinners had been billed to Leonard's account. He had had no other guests billed to him that week.

The county detective felt that a fairly accurate picture of how Dean had got hold of the bonds was beginning to emerge. He was the guest billed to

Riggott on April 12. At the latter's apartment the conversation must have turned to the trip Riggott was tentatively planning. It reminded him that his passport needed to be renewed and he took it from the safe in Dean's presence. Then, after Loretta Madler called, he left Dean alone with the safe. Either he hadn't locked it properly before he left, or else Dean had been able to figure out the combination through watching him work it. While Riggott was absent he got the safe open and stole the bonds.

Riggott must have mentioned how little he kept in it. Since he had removed his passport from it he would, in all likelihood, have no occasion to open it again in the near future.

However, he had changed his plans and wouldn't be using his passport. When he picked it up at the travel agency and went to put it back in the safe he found the bonds missing. With the incident of opening it in front of Dean still fresh in his mind, he had known right away the young man was the thief.

Apparently, from his call to Jim, he hadn't wanted to go to the police at once. He didn't even want to see Jim until the next day. The delay indicated a time ultimatum given to Dean. If you return what you stole from me by such and such a time, we'll keep the whole thing quiet. If you don't, I'll take it to the county detective. I know him personally. He's a neighbor of mine at the lake.

That was how it had probably gone, Jim thought. Dean had used the time margin to set the stage for the murder.

He went to Goodrich with this latest product of his reasoning. Goodrich thought it was sound; it looked

209

like a good answer to their problem of how Dean had got hold of the bonds. After they had discussed it the state's attorney inquired, "Have you heard anything from the Bureau yet about his car?"

"No."

"Why not try to rush them along a little?"

"I'll see what I can do." Jim went back to his office. He had no intention of harrying the Identification Bureau. They knew he wanted their report as soon as possible. When it was ready they'd call him.

He dropped down in his chair and turned his thoughts to the Iver-Johnson that had killed Riggott. In the inquiry he had sent through to the Philadelphia police yesterday he had emphasized his need to find out if Dean had even mentioned owning a gun to any of his friends even though it was not registered.

If he had acquired the gun legitimately, it hadn't been done since his arrival in Hampton. Every .22 Iver-Johnson target pistol listed with the state police gun-permit division as having been bought within the past year had been followed up. The murder weapon itself had been given all sorts of publicity. But no one had come forward with information about it.

Jim placed himself in Dean's position last April faced with a sudden need to kill Riggott. He'd been very busy the night before he did it; he couldn't have been looking for a gun at the same time.

He must have already had the gun in his possession. There were a number of ways to get hold of one without registering for it.

The attempt to link Dean with the Iver-Johnson looked hopeless. Nevertheless, Jim meant to go ahead with it. He had to begin somewhere; he would begin with Elaine.

He went to see her at her third-floor furnished apartment in what had once been a private home. She received him coldly. He represented a threat to the wonderful gift Leonard Riggott had made to Dean.

When her husband had told her about it last night her resentment over not having been told sooner was lost in delight over the gift itself. She believed what he told her; she wanted to believe every word of it.

Jim, feeling his way along, realized what a limited version of the affair she had heard from Dean. He listened to her questions concerning Dean's prospects of keeping the bonds and said yes, if her husband could prove they were a gift from Riggott he would be allowed to keep them.

"I'm sure he can," Elaine declared, with the first smile she had bestowed on Jim since he entered the apartment. "Of course they were a gift. How else could he have got them?"

She went on to talk about what a difference the money was going to make in their lives and the things they would do with it. She was amoral, Jim reflected. She didn't really care how Dean had come into possession of the bonds as long as he had them. Money was her god, everything she wanted from life could be bought with it.

He was sitting in an easy chair. On the table beside it lay magazines, a pencil, an ash tray. His glance strayed to the magazines and sharpened as it settled on the cover of one of them. Someone had doodled on it and he remembered at once where he had seen that particular doodle before. While Elaine wasn't looking he slid the magazine under his coat.

He let her talk a little longer about her plans for the future, but he didn't listen to a word she said. He was too conscious of the weighty piece of evidence he held pressed against his side.

When he inserted the question he had come to ask his tone was almost perfunctory: "What kind of a gun does Dean own?"

"Gun?" Elaine's astonishment was genuine, Jim felt. She had no knowledge of the murder weapon. Dean hadn't had it around since her arrival in Hampton; he'd got rid of it long before that.

Elaine's reaction time was slow. It took her a moment to grasp what the county detective's question implied. In reply she told him to get out of her apartment. "You're desperate," she cried. "You're trying to implicate Dean or anyone you can to save your own face."

Jim didn't answer. She followed him to the door, accusations pouring from her in a bitter flow. He said, "Good-by, Mrs. Lipscomb," and closed the door after him.

He showed the magazine to Goodrich and phoned the Identification Bureau about the other doodle he had seen. It would become a major exhibit in the case of the State versus Dean Lipscomb.

Cobb returned from New York late in the afternoon. He had with him the bonds and the Atlantic certificate.

While he was telling Jim about his trip a call came in from the Identification Bureau. The officer who was calling said, "We've got a couple of things for you, Mr. O'Neill. We've been making comparison tests on the fuzz we vacuumed out of the trunk of the car you sent over and the fuzz that was found on Riggott's clothing.

Both came from an army blanket of the same dye lot and both came from a blanket that was quite new. We can start tracing it back to the manufacturer, but that will take time, you know. Then we found a hemlock needle in the trunk. Same variety as the ones that were caught in the sole of Riggott's shoe. It's Eastern hemlock which is, of course, found everywhere around here. Even so—"

"Yes," Jim said, "it's corroborative." He thanked the officer and hung up.

When he told Goodrich what the Bureau had reported the latter said, "Do you want to bring him in right now for further questioning?"

"We haven't heard from Philadelphia yet," Jim pointed out. "I have no real hope of their getting a line on the gun, but why not let Lipscomb sweat it out tonight and tackle him in the morning? He's being tailed. He won't get away."

The state's attorney agreed that they might as well do what Jim suggested.

The gun was foremost in the latter's mind as he went back to his own office. There was some possibility connected with it that kept eluding him; he couldn't quite pin it down in his thoughts. It had nothing to do with the report that would come from the Philadelphia police. That would be negative as far as the Iver-Johnson was concerned. If it could be traced to him in Philadelphia, Dean wouldn't have dared to use it.

Some other possibility . . .

The county detective sat down at his desk. Deliberately he gave his attention to the morals case on which he had been working concurrently with the murder. Then, after he had dismissed the possibility connected with the gun from his mind, it came back into it full-fledged. He reached for the telephone and called the communications officer at state police headquarters. He had another inquiry to send out.

Cobb brought Dean to Jim's office at nine o'clock the next morning. By that time the county detective had heard from the Philadelphia police. They reported that Dean's family background was good, but that he was considered overindulged and irresponsible. He had been involved in various minor escapades as a youth although none of them had wound up in Juvenile Court. He had lost his job at an insurance agency where he had been employed before going to Hampton. According to what the police had been able to find out, his dismissal had something to do with a falsified check. Since the insurance agency had brought no charges it was assumed Dean's father had made good whatever sum of money was involved. No one the police had questioned among Dean's acquaintance knew of his ever having owned a gun.

This was all the additional information Jim had on the young man when the latter walked into his office at nine o'clock with Cobb beside him.

There were deep circles under Dean's eyes. His face had lost much of its boyishness in the last two days. He moved like someone in a dream.

He hadn't, after all, engaged a lawyer. To do so he would have to talk about what was happening to him; talking about it would give it reality, and that was the one thing his situation mustn't be allowed to acquire.

Yesterday, when he returned from New York, Elaine had been waiting with news of Jim's visit, his question about a gun. Dean had brushed it aside. It was all straightened out now, he said, they'd have the bonds back in a few days. There was nothing to worry about.

He had kept repeating the same thing to himself during the sleepless hours of the night. Then, this morning, half an hour ago, Cobb had arrived at his door and announced that Jim wanted to see him again.

Dean knew he should insist on a lawyer right away, but he didn't do it. He had frozen himself fast in his role of a man with a clear conscience who had nothing to fear from the police beyond the inconvenience of answering questions that were based on a misunderstanding.

He sat down in the chair Jim indicated and essayed a smile. "I hope we can get this thing cleared up today, Mr. O'Neill."

The county detective replied, "Well, there are some questions . . ."

Again he took Dean through his story of Leonard's giving him the bonds. He moved on to the next time Dean had seen the dead man.

"It must have been Monday or Tuesday of the week he died," Dean informed him.

Jim toyed with the paper knife on his desk. He said briefly, "You saw him the day he put his passport back in the safe and found the bonds missing—the day he called me."

The county detective's knowledge of the passport incident was an unexpected blow. Dean went white from it, but he kept his voice firm in denial. "I know nothing about his passport. He never mentioned it to me."

"He took it out of his safe in front of you the night of April 12 when you were at his apartment. That's how you got at the bonds."

"Indeed not! He gave them to me."

Jim flung dates at him; the date the passport was taken to Watson's, the date Riggott picked it up there, the same date he pointed out, that Riggott had called him, the county detective. Then he outlined the whole procedure of the murder, including the fact that Dean had left the body in the trunk of his car until he placed it in the cottage.

"No," Dean kept saying. "No, no—"

Jim sat back in his chair. "The day before yesterday your car was examined by the Identification Bureau. In the trunk were bits of fuzz from an army blanket that matched the fuzz found on Riggott's clothing."

Dean looked ghastly. Well, he said, he'd once had an army blanket and he'd kept it in his trunk.

"Where did you buy it?"

"Why—in New York. Three or four years ago."

"Where is it now?"

"I don't know what became of it. I lost it, left it somewhere."

"When did you lose it?"

Dean, remembering that he'd owned his present car only a few months, avoided the hazard Jim's question offered by replying, "Early this summer. Around the first part of June."

Jim brought up the hemlock needles. Dean said he'd spread his blanket on the ground many times; he could have picked up anything on it.

He had an answer to everything, a preternatural sharpness of mind this morning. His life was at stake.

At nine-thirty Goodrich arrived and began to take part in the questioning. Cobb sat off to one side taking notes.

Jim and the state's attorney spelled each other, varying the pace, throwing questions at Dean rapidly for a while, then letting silences fall.

His glance darted from one to the other. Sweat poured from him, his face was bloodless. But they couldn't shake his story.

A few minutes before noon Jim received a call from state police headquarters. The communications officer said, "A message just came in for you from the Providence police. Dean Lipscomb bought a .22 Iver-Johnson target pistol at Keene's sporting-goods shop in Providence on May 3, 1946."

"Well," said Jim, and then in heartfelt tones, "Thanks very much."

He hung up and contemplated Dean with something near benevolence. The young man himself had led the county detective to the gun. His practice of telling as much of the truth as possible had brought his uncle in Providence into the explanation he had given Tad of where he would get the money to buy stock. Last night Jim, remembering the uncle, had sent off his inquiry to the Providence police.

He said, "I believe you told us you didn't bring back a gun from North Africa."

"No, I didn't."

"You've never owned a gun?"

"I'm not particularly interested in them. I've never owned one."

"What about the Iver-Johnson you shot Riggott with?"

"I didn't shoot him. And I've never owned an Iver-Johnson."

217

"Haven't you?" Jim's tone hardened. "You're a consistent liar, it seems. I just got a message from the Providence police about the Iver-Johnson you bought there in May 1946."

Dean's jaw went slack. The room began to whirl around him. He'd known they'd check in Philadelphia for a gun, but Providence—who'd ever expect—? All those years ago when he'd worked there one summer—the target shooting he'd done—

He'd left the gun at his uncle Ike's packed in a suitcase with an old tennis racket that needed restringing, a broken camera, a few other odds and ends. He'd almost forgotten it until he visited his uncle last March and the latter suggested he take the suitcase back to Hampton with him. He hadn't even opened it until he brought it to the rooming house. His uncle hadn't known the gun was in it—no one knew—

Dean's breath came fast. Should he deny ownership of it, say it must be some other Dean Lipscomb? No, that was no good, he thought despairingly. They'd compare his signature on the registration form with samples of his handwriting . . .

What should he say?

The silence spun itself out unbearably. The three pairs of eyes, Cobb's, Jim's, Goodrich's, were fastened on him. He had to say something.

His tongue licked his lips. "Yes, I bought that gun," he said in a high, crackling voice. "I lied about it. If I hadn't, you'd have been down on me like a ton of bricks."

"Where is your Iver-Johnson?" Jim asked.

"I haven't the faintest idea. I didn't take it with me when I left Providence and I don't recall ever seeing it

218

again." Dean's glance flickered over the group. Disbelief was on the three faces.

Jim led him through his story of the gun repeatedly. Each time it had a feebler ring.

Then they dropped the gun for the moment and took him back to other parts of his story. They were tireless. Dean became more and more confused. He resorted to bluster. "I've said all I'm going to say until I get a lawyer."

"You were going to get one the other day," Goodrich observed. "Why haven't you done it?"

"Because I knew I was innocent and I felt that you people would give me fair treatment. I was wrong about that and I now refuse to answer any more questions until I get a lawyer." Dean took courage from the sound of his own voice charged with righteous wrath. "I can see what you're up to. You've got a few coincidences to work on and you're trying to build them into a case that's based on nothing but circumstantial evidence."

"Don't ever decry that," Goodrich said gently. "It's of vital importance. It convicts people time after time. Why shouldn't it? A man who's engaged in an unlawful activity isn't going to go out of his way to supply an eyewitness to his crime. It's up to the police to gather circumstantial evidence against him. And in your case, Mr. Lipscomb, there's a good bit of it."

The state's attorney proceeded to summarize it; the bonds that had supplied a motive for murder, the gun, the discrepancies in Dean's story, the admissions wrung from him. He talked at length about the bits of fuzz in the trunk of Dean's car, how they would be traced back to the manufacturer and eventually would

expose Dean's lie about having bought the blanket i
New York three or four years ago. "The Bureau says it'
a fairly new blanket," Goodrich stated. "They'll trac
down the very shipment it was sent out in. It will be on
that was sent to. Hampton during the past year or sc
not one that was sent to New York three or four year
ago."

Dean had three handkerchiefs with him today an
they had all been reduced to wet balls. He wiped hi
face with one of them and stared defiantly at Goodrich
and Jim. "I didn't kill him. I had no gun. I haven't seer
mine for years. I didn't put his body in his cottage. I'v
never set foot in it in my life."

There was a frenzied note in his voice. The count
detective judged that it was time to get in the finishin
stroke. He began, "You've never set foot in Riggott'
cottage in your life, to say nothing of having killed hin
and placed his body there?"

"That's right." Dean gave him a hunted look. "Yes
that's exactly right."

"Never in your life?"

Dean sensed a land mine about to explode anc
destroy him. But he had committed himself. He had tc
embrace his own destruction. "Never in my life," he
said.

"Then how did your signature get there?"

"My—signature?"

"Well, that's what I'd call it. A doodle scratched on
the window sill of Riggott's cottage. Something kept
you there the day you brought in the body—some time
element, perhaps—and you were under such tension I
don't suppose you realized what you were doing. I've
seen you fooling with that penknife you use for

220

craping out your pipe. That day you doodled with it."

"A few scratches on a window sill—" Dean eyed him wildly. "Anyone could have—"

"No, not this doodle. It was your signature, the Greek letters for Sigma Pi, your college fraternity. They're on the window sill at the cottage and on the cover of a magazine I picked up at your apartment yesterday. We'll have that window sill cut right out of the frame. It will become a state exhibit at your trial."

A wordless cry broke from Dean followed by dead silence. He clutched at his stomach. Suddenly the accumulated strain of the past few days had settled in it. He dove for the lavatory off Jim's office and was violently sick.

After that there was no resistance left in him. He lay like a boneless rag on the leather sofa in Jim's office, drinking carton after carton of black coffee, finding relief from all strain in telling them in fullest detail about the murder of Leonard Riggott.

It was six o'clock that night when Jim left him at the county jail. He had telephoned Phoebe Beecher. She was with Elaine.

He stood looking after Dean as the latter was led away to a cell. He regarded a murderer as a job to be done only until he was behind bars. Then he became a person again to Jim. In this case, a young man who had seemed pleasant and likable and who faced indictment on a charge of first-degree murder.

But Leonard Riggott had been a person too . . .

Jim shook his head and left. It was good to get in his car and start home to Margaret and the children, to look forward to his vacation next week as a respite from the dark patterns of crime.

THE BESTSELLING NOVELS
BEHIND THE BLOCKBUSTER MOVIES —
ZEBRA'S MOVIE MYSTERY GREATS!

HIGH SIERRA (2059, $3.50)
by W.R. Burnett
A dangerous criminal on the lam is trapped in a terrifying web of circumstance. The tension-packed novel that inspired the 1955 film classic starring Humphrey Bogart and directed by John Houston.

MR. ARKADIN (2145, $3.50)
by Orson Welles
A playboy's search to uncover the secrets of financier Gregory Arkadin's hidden past exposes a worldwide intrigue of big money, corruption — and murder. Orson Welles's only novel, and the basis for the acclaimed film written by, directed by, and starring himself.

NOBODY LIVES FOREVER (2217, $3.50)
by W.R. Burnett
Jim Farrar's con game backfires when his beautiful victim lures him into a dangerous deception that could only end in death. A 1946 cinema classic starring John Garfield and Geraldine Fitzgerald. (AVAILABLE IN FEBRUARY 1988)

BUILD MY GALLOWS HIGH (2341, $3.50)
by Geoffrey Homes
When Red Bailey's former lover Mumsie McGonigle lured him from the Nevada hills back to the deadly hustle of New York City, the last thing the ex-detective expected was to be set up as a patsy and framed for a murder he didn't commit. The novel that inspired the screen gem OUT OF THE PAST, starring Robert Mitchum and Kirk Douglas. (AVAILABLE IN APRIL 1988)

Available wherever paperbacks are sold, or order direct from the Publisher. Send cover price plus 50¢ per copy for mailing and handling to Zebra Books, Dept. 2286, 475 Park Avenue South, New York, N.Y. 10016. Residents of New York, New Jersey and Pennsylvania must include sales tax. DO NOT SEND CASH.